THREE FOR A GIRL

A Magpie Romantic Suspense Mystery

Marlow Kelly

Viceroy Press

ISBN: 978-1-9991430-8-4

Edited by Corinne Demaagd
From CMD Writing and Editing
https://cmdediting.com

Proofreading by
Gemma Brocato
https://www.gemmabrocato.com

For news of Marlow's next book sign up for Marlow's Newsletter
at: www.marlowkelly.com

CHAPTER ONE

This wasn't the first dead body Randy Woychuk had discovered, but it was the most shocking. He never imagined he would find a corpse in his hometown of Magpie.

He was up early because he hadn't been able to sleep. His amputated leg hurt like a bitch. Why an appendage that had been severed two years ago would still cause him pain was a mystery. He'd waited until dawn and then driven to an isolated spot in the marshy wetlands along the shore of Charm Lake.

This had been his favorite place to "park" when he was in high school. It was perfect. The golf course next door was closed at night, so no one would bother them. And they were far enough from the town's light pollution they could see the stars. On a good night, the northern lights put on a show. It was as if the aurora borealis was as excited by their lovemaking as they were.

This morning would probably be his last time here. A couple of property developers had petitioned the government of Alberta to delist the parkland so they could build condos.

Damn. Some of his best memories were here with... He dragged his mind away from the past. It wouldn't do any good to look back.

There would be no beautiful sunrise with orange and pink streaks across the sky today. The clouds hung heavy, darkening the morning. Fluffy white snow swirled in the breeze. It wasn't falling heavy enough to accumulate, but it added to his somber mood.

He pulled a pack of cigarettes from his jacket pocket. He hated smoking, despised the weakness his nicotine addiction represented, but it was better than drinking his trauma away. He turned and flicked his lighter, shielding the small flame from the east wind and light snow. That's when he saw her, floating like a swollen, skin-colored log. *Shit.*

He splashed through the muddy water, ignoring the icy late-October cold. His heart thudded hard against his ribcage. He was waist deep by the time he reached her. There was a misshapen mass where she'd been struck on the back of her head. He turned her over. Another wound marred her face. They were clearly visible despite her bloated, lifeless appearance. She wore a pale blue sweater and jeans with a cheap yellow rope tied around her waist. He knew her. He couldn't remember her name, but he'd seen her in town. She used to be a waitress at the Rockin Horse.

He scanned the area but couldn't see anyone. He stilled, listening for any sound that would indicate there was someone else nearby, but there was nothing except the ripple of the water and the wakening birds.

He backed away, not sure if he was disturbing evidence. He'd seen cop shows on television, but that was fiction. He needed to call the police. Okay, that was a solid plan. His phone was in his truck. He retraced his steps, trying to walk out of the lake the way he'd come in, not because of police procedure, but the silty floor was uneven. He didn't want to get his prosthesis stuck in an underwater hole.

Dripping wet, he stumbled through the mud, every movement seeming to take a lifetime. Finally, he climbed into the driver's seat, turned on the engine, and blasted the heat. His hands were shaking when he reached into the glove compartment for his phone. He knew from experience his reaction was a combination of being physically cold and the adrenalin spike from finding someone dead.

The emergency operator answered on the second ring.

"I found the body of a young woman. She's been murdered."

CHAPTER TWO

George Scott lay in bed with her body tucked against Liam's side and her head on his shoulder. Waking up and making love to him was the highlight of her day. It was all downhill after that. She tried to keep a routine, but she was just going through the motions, working to keep herself busy rather than being a productive member of society.

Liam seemed to enjoy his new role as chief of the Magpie Police Service. He'd been offered the job two months ago, but before that, he'd been a corporal with the RCMP, working undercover. She ran her fingers through his chest hair. The lack of excitement, the paperwork, and day-to-day routine of the position didn't seem to get to him. But it did get to her.

Actually, that was a lie. It wasn't his job that bothered her. It was her own lack of work. She'd been officially diagnosed with epilepsy at the end of August. She used to fill her time by helping out at the local food bank but had quit because the other volunteers didn't see her as a regular civilian. Almost every day one of them had complained to her about their neighbour's barking dog, street parking, or a house party. They still pictured her as a cop and thought she could sort it all out, but she couldn't. In the end, she'd given up her charity work.

She sighed, rolled toward her night table, and opened her prescription pill bottle. She swallowed a capsule and chased it with a glass of water she kept by the bed for that purpose. "Do you think I'll always have to take these?"

"Yes." He rolled so his front was against her back, his softening penis poking her bare butt. He placed his hand on her stomach. "Do they still make you feel nauseous?"

"Not as bad as when I started taking them." Her anti-seizure medication could produce numerous side effects but, luckily, she'd only experienced an upset stomach.

"Do you blame me for the epilepsy?" His words were barely a whisper.

She disentangled herself from his embrace and sat up, wanting to see his expression. "Why would you think that?"

"Because I tackled you. I knocked you to the ground, and your head hit the sidewalk. That injury caused your condition." He frowned, the lines around his mouth deepening as he stared into the distance, not meeting her gaze.

She cupped his face, his stubble in the morning nearly as long as his short-cropped brown hair. "Look at me," she demanded.

He did as he was told, shifting his dark gaze toward her.

"It was never your fault. I chose to be a cop. We had a job to do, and part of that was apprehending a naked man who was high on angel dust. He wasn't a big guy, but he managed to lift me off the ground. You had no choice but to tackle him. If anyone's to blame, it's Hank Scott."

"Your father?"

"He's the one who sold the guy the marijuana laced with PCP. If he hadn't done that, none of this would've happened. You and I were collateral damage."

He reached up and slid his fingers into her hair, cradling her head. At the same time, he drew her to him, so she was lying on top of his chest. His mouth covered hers.

She reciprocated, dipping her tongue between his teeth. In that moment, she forgot about everything: her epilepsy, her lack of work, and her boredom. Nothing mattered except the man in her bed.

She broke the kiss, trailing her fingers along his side until she reached the dent of his hip bone. "How much time do you have?"

He rested his forehead against hers. "Not enough."

"Then you should get out of bed now before I convince you to submit to my will." She waggled her eyebrows.

He laughed as he jumped out of bed and headed for the bathroom. "It wouldn't take much convincing."

She watched him walk away, enjoying the way his muscles moved under the smooth skin of his buttocks.

He turned. "Hey, eyes up here." He waved two fingers at his face, telling her where to look. "A man wants to be appreciated for his mind, too."

She grinned. "I do. I'm just multitasking."

He chuckled as he closed the door.

She stretched and then grabbed her warm, fuzzy robe. With Liam's body heat gone, she could feel the chill in the air. It was the last week of October, and already the temperature was dipping close to -10 Celsius. She padded to the kitchen and poured her favorite blend of coffee beans into the grinder.

She could stay home all day. Or she could catch a ride into town with him, work out at the gym, and then have coffee at the Jumping Bean Café with her friend Olivia. That would fill her morning, at least.

It had been two months since her last seizure, and she was paralysed by indecision. Liam wanted to move into town, which made sense and was a good idea. With no license and only her bike—a bike her friend Buddy had loaned her—she had no transportation.

They'd toured a few places with a view to renting, but none of them had grabbed her. She didn't like any of the apartments because they made her feel cramped. They'd also looked at two houses, both of which were nicer and bigger than the home they currently occupied, but she'd rejected them. The first one was filthy with mold growing everywhere. There was no way she was living in that. She hadn't liked the second home because it was in the center of town and was overlooked by an apartment building. She couldn't picture herself living in any of the places they'd seen, which was probably nuts on her part because she needed to be in Magpie.

She stared out the window. The light snow had dissipated, and the sun was rising over the lake. It would be a sunny, crisp day.

Her biggest problem was that she was no longer a productive member of society. She'd spent all her adult life trying to help others. Now she was adrift.

Liam entered the kitchen and stood behind her, looping his arms around her waist, drawing her into his embrace. She sighed as she savored his clean scent and the feel of his body against hers. "That's good."

He bent his head and laid small pecks along her neck. "I wish I had more time," he whispered between kisses.

"Me, too." She wanted to drag him back to bed and enjoy the feel of his long length inside her. Sex was a great distraction from her problems.

He straightened. "I have a meeting with the mayor and the town council at eight."

She nodded and heaved another sigh. "I know." He had told her about the appointment, but she'd forgotten. There was no way she would be ready in time to catch a ride without making him late.

He grabbed a travel mug from the cupboard. He looked good in his uniform, a black shirt and tie and black pants with a red stripe down the outside seam. He shrugged into his thick winter uniform jacket, which was also black with a Magpie Police Service patch on the arm. Concern flickered in his dark eyes as his lips pressed into a thin line. "What do you plan to do today?"

He knew she was struggling, and although he hadn't pushed, he also needed her to make decisions about their living arrangements and her work situation. She couldn't stay home, staring at the walls all day every day.

"I'm going to see if there are any new listings for lease or rent." She didn't mention walking into town in the cold because it would only worry him, and he didn't need that.

He crossed the living room then turned and blew her a kiss when he reached the front door. "Wish me luck with the bean counters."

"Good luck, but you won't need it. Last year's budget wasn't under your control. They know that."

His phone buzzed, and he fished it out of his inside jacket pocket. "What's up?"

She couldn't hear what was being said, but Liam's dark eyes

widened. "I'm on my way."

He dashed out of the house without another word.

She watched from the window as he hopped down the steps and headed for her old Subaru. The cold didn't seem to affect him at all.

She stepped back out of his view as he started the car. Whatever the phone call was about, he wasn't inclined to share, which was not a surprise. Some cases were restricted. Information was only shared with those officers directly involved. It wouldn't be appropriate for him to tell her.

She'd shower, put on her warmest layers of clothing, and walk into town. Working out at the gym and then visiting her friend Olivia at the Jumping Bean would give her something to do.

CHAPTER THREE

Liam watched as Sergeant Mia Olsen pulled up in a RCMP-issue Ford SUV. She wore her uniform of a navy jacket, beige shirt, and matching pants with a distinctive yellow stripe running down the outside seam. Her long blond hair was tied back in some sort of braid. She looked pissed.

The Royal Canadian Mounted Police had taken control of the scene. The Magpie Police Service were a community force. Violent crimes, especially those involving an unexpected death, were normally investigated by the RCMP, a federal police force who also worked in various towns, cities, and municipalities throughout Canada. The Mounties would have the body delivered to the Office of the Chief Medical Examiner for an autopsy.

Liam's small group of police officers were simply acting as gatekeepers, allowing only those on official business into the taped-off area.

As Magpie Police Chief, he was just here to observe and offer assistance. He gritted his teeth against the icy breeze. He'd been living in Alberta for a couple of years and was used to the frigid winters, but the biting wind always got to him.

Luckily, Randy Woychuk, the man who had found the body, had stayed at the scene, even though he was soaking wet. He sat in his truck, drinking a cup of coffee. Liam had his workout clothes, which he kept in his locker at work, delivered here. Liam was an inch shorter than Randy, but he figured his dirty sweats were better than Randy freezing his butt off while waiting for the RCMP to question him.

No sightseers had driven here from town, which was good. But the manager of the golf course next door watched from a spot next to a Magpie police cruiser. Liam remembered his name was James Stilton, but the only reason he'd retained that bit of information was because he thought Stilton was a cheesy name. At the time, he'd silently laughed at his own joke, which he knew wasn't really funny.

Why Stilton felt the need to be present was a mystery. He stood huddled in his down coat with his hood pulled up over his bald head, watching the proceedings. Maybe he'd been working at the golf course and had come to see what the fuss was about.

Mia marched toward Liam. "Do you know the identity of the victim?"

He flipped open his notepad. "We don't have an official ID, but we believe the victim is Carly Hale. She's twenty-two and completing the last year of her Bachelor's Degree in Education at the University of Alberta. She was also a waitress at the Rockin Horse before it closed. That is, when she was home from school."

Mia dug a book from her back pocket and unclipped a pen from the binding. "After the Rockin Horse?" She obviously remembered that the bar had closed down when the owner, Mattie Rogers, had killed Smokie, a resident of Magpie, and then tried to poison Georgina.

Liam cleared his throat and then said, "She was a housekeeper at the Charm Hotel. She was the one who gave us the key to the journalist's room last summer."

"Reading between the lines, your girlfriend knows her." She scribbled down that detail.

"They're not close, but yes," Liam admitted.

"I'm surprised she's not here." Mia arched a questioning eyebrow.

"Who, Georgina?" Although she had a gift for solving crimes, seeing death made her sick to her stomach. He was grateful she wouldn't see her friend this way. "I haven't told her. I'm trying to keep a lid on it until we can notify Carly's family. Not that Georgina would say anything." His frustration, he realized, wasn't with Mia or the RCMP but with himself because he didn't have the power to take control of the case. Liam pointed to Randy. "See that guy sitting in the truck?"

"What about him?" Mia turned, taking in the beat-up Ford pickup and the man with shoulder-length scruffy brown hair behind the wheel.

"He discovered Carly. He's ex-army. Lost his lower leg. He's wearing my dirty sweats because his clothes got wet when he ran into the lake to retrieve her."

"Do you think he's a suspect?"

"I'm trying not to think anything. He said he came down here to see the place one last time before it's turned into condos."

"Do you believe him?"

Liam assessed Randy. For some reason, he felt a kinship with the burned-out ex-soldier. "Yes, and I'd consider it a personal favor if you could interview him and get him out of here."

She gave him an incredulous look. "Maybe we should hold him on suspicion. What if he takes off?"

"I think he would love to take off, but he's got nowhere else to go. That's why he's living at his parents' farm." Liam had learned in his first two months as police chief that getting to know the problems, hopes, and concerns of the people of Magpie helped him in his job more than any police procedure ever could.

Mia nodded and strode over to her car to talk to the officers who were huddled, chatting. Liam didn't recognize them, but that didn't mean anything. He'd quit the RCMP months ago, and things changed quickly.

A female officer in uniform nodded at Mia's command and strode over to talk to Randy.

Mia returned to his side. "Satisfied?"

"Thanks."

"Tell me more about the victim."

"Hold on a sec." Liam held up a hand in a halt motion. "Greg," he called, waving his officer over. "This is Constable Nicholson," he said to Mia. Greg Nicholson wasn't Liam's fittest officer, but he was honest and cared about the community. "He's known the family the longest." Then Liam addressed Greg. "Can you please tell Sergeant Olsen what you told me about Carly?"

"I wrote down everything I can remember." Greg cleared his

throat as he tugged his notebook out of his pocket. "She grew up in Magpie. The only daughter to a single mother. Her mom's name is Susan Hale. She supports the family as a cleaning lady, which doesn't sound like much, but word is she charges a lot and has a full schedule of customers. She's also in demand with those who have cabins in the area. Carly turned twenty-two last January. I looked that up. She went to school here and then to university in Edmonton. She still came home for the summers. George might know more about her social life and who her friends are. Neither Carly nor her mother have ever been in trouble with the police." Greg stuffed his notebook back into his pocket. "Oh, and one last point. If she was working as a student teacher, she would've had a criminal record check and her fingerprints would've been taken. It might help with her official identification."

"Thanks, Greg. Great job." Liam watched as Nicholson returned to his post as gatekeeper. "Do you want me to call Georgina?" he asked Mia.

She nodded. "Might as well."

****

George tugged her hat down over her ears, shielding them from the cold as she walked along the lakeshore. Light snow swirled around her, driven by the wind. She would've liked to focus on the birds, but she had to keep an eye on the path. Being this close to the water meant the pathways could get damp and ice up. She didn't want to slip. She had enough on her plate without a twisted ankle, or worse.

Her phone rang, and she fished it out of her pocket. A photo of Liam appeared on the screen. "How's it going?"

He gave a deep sigh, a sign that he was having a bad day. "There's no easy way to say this... Carly's dead."

"Carly? Young Carly?"

"The waitress from the Rockin Horse, yes."

"What happened? Was there an accident?" It had to be. The roads froze and got slick at this time of year. People weren't used

11

to winter driving this early in the season; some hadn't even put on their snow tires yet.

"It's a homicide."

Liam's words echoed through her skull, but she couldn't seem to equate his statement with reality. "Who would want to kill her? Was it random? A joke that went wrong? What happened?"

"We don't know. But I have to talk to the people who knew her, so I thought I'd start with you."

"Has her mom been notified?" For the first time since her diagnosis, George was grateful she was on sick leave. Susan Hale was a sweet woman whose world was about to be shattered.

"No. The RCMP are handling that. I'll go with them. We're waiting for an official ID, and then we'll get someone from Victim Services to join us."

"Shit."

"Is there anything you can tell us?"

"Not really. I know her because she worked for Mattie." George gazed out at the lake, the reeds bending in the wind. In her mind, she pictured Carly at the Rockin Horse, doing her homework on her break. "She was a hard worker."

"Greg said she wanted to be a teacher." Liam seemed detached and efficient.

"She was so sweet." George's voice cracked. She didn't want to break down and give into the emotion, but the death of someone so young, and so good, hit her like a physical blow.

"I'm sorry."

She straightened, pulling herself together, sniffling back her tears. "No, it's okay. How are you holding up?"

"Fine." It was a one-word answer, which conveyed a feeling rather than a fact. He wasn't fine. Seeing the body of a young woman would get to anyone, but he was coping because he had a job to do.

After a long pause, he asked, "What can you tell me about her personal life?"

"Nothing." Someone had killed her. *God.* George clutched her phone a little tighter. "We talked about school or work. She'd taken out a student loan to pay for her education, and she asked me how long it took to pay back. I advised her on how to handle her professors. I gave her some tips on staying safe in the city because I didn't want..." She inhaled a calming breath. She could fall apart later. "I guess talking about her finances is pretty personal, but I don't know about anything that could've gotten her killed. To be honest, I didn't see much of her once the Rockin Horse closed down. The last time we met, I was with you at the Charm Hotel."

"Okay, thanks." He was silent for a moment and then said, "You won't tell anyone?"

"No." Part of her was insulted that he'd asked, but she let it go. It was too important for him to take the risk. "I'll talk to you tonight." She disconnected and shoved the phone back in her pocket. She turned on her heel and headed back the way she'd come. She didn't want to socialize. She wanted to go home and cry

CHAPTER FOUR

George sat on her shabby couch with her feet up on her re-finished coffee table, cradling a mug in her hands. She'd arrived home over an hour ago, and she still wasn't warm. There was housework to do, but she couldn't face it. Moving was just too much effort. The news of Carly's death had shaken her to her core.

A knock on the front door startled her. George placed her mug on the coffee table. No one had knocked in months. Her sister and friends texted before they visited. She grabbed her baseball bat from its place in the corner and peered through the glass window. Randy Woychuk stared back at her. *What the hell?* Randy was ex-army who lived on his parent's farm west of town. The last time she'd met him he'd seemed pretty pissed off, which was not surprising since she'd been at his farm to inter-rogate him.

She flung open the door with her bat ready. "Hi, Randy, what can I do for you?"

He rubbed his face and then turned around seeming to stare at some imaginary figure behind him. After a pause, he swung back to her. "Have you talked to Liam?"

"Yes."

"Then you know." He looked down at his hands, which were clasped together so tightly his knuckles were white.

"Know what?" She refused to reveal any information. She didn't know Randy well, and this might be a fishing expedition.

"I found Carly." He shook his head slightly, as if denying the truth, but his red-rimmed eyes revealed his anguish.

"Maybe you should come in." She placed her bat back in the corner. "Can I get you a coffee?"

"No, thanks." He shook his head as he stepped inside.

A wonderful aroma that mingled with cigarette smoke

wafted after him, which was disconcerting. She wasn't attracted to Randy at all, so why should his odor be so appealing?

With his left hand, he shoved his unkempt red-brown hair out of his eyes and sat in the armchair by the window. "You're not seeing me at my best."

"You've had a tough morning." She stood by the door, shocked by her own physical response.

"I don't suppose I can smoke in here." He held a pack of cigarettes and a lighter in his right hand.

"On the deck." That would get him out of the house where his smell could dissipate, and then maybe she could concentrate.

She hadn't stored her outdoor furniture yet, which consisted of two cheap chairs and a matching coffee table, which wasn't a big job. Her failure to put them in her shed was laziness on her part, but now worked in her favor. She stepped back as he limped past her again. His artificial right leg was visible just below the hem of his green sweatpants, which had the letters *UBC* emblazoned along the side. "UBC for University of British Columbia? Are those Liam's clothes?"

"Yeah. It was a choice between his dry gym gear or my soaking wet jeans." He collapsed into a plastic chair, shook a cigarette out of the pack, and lit it.

Mystery solved. It wasn't Randy's scent that intoxicated her; it was Liam's. Which was a relief because it meant the world made sense again. "That's not much of a choice. Is your leg bothering you?" His limp wasn't normally this pronounced.

"Everything got wet. It's caused some chafing." He took a long drag of his smoke.

"How are your parents?" She shrugged into her coat and sat next to him, planting her feet on the railing.

"Fine. They're spending the winter in Osoyoos in British Columbia."

"That sounds nice." She inwardly growled, the small talk getting to her.

"They want to sell the farm." His voice was flat, devoid of any emotion.

"Will you buy it?"

He shrugged. "I have no idea what I should do next."

"I can relate to that."

He pressed his lips into a thin line. "Sorry about the epilepsy."

She said nothing, not wanting to discuss her condition with him—a wounded veteran she hardly knew who was smoking on her deck. "What brings you here?"

"Come with me to see Carly's mom? I need to pay my respects."

"No." There was no way she wanted to deal with a bereaved mother. There was nothing she, or anyone, could say to make up for the loss of a child. "We don't even know if the police have notified her yet. We can't go until then."

He gave a slow nod as he acknowledged her words. "Okay. That's fair, but we have to go."

"Why?" Maybe it was cowardly on her part, but she didn't want to deal with Susan Hale's grief. "We can pay our respects at her funeral."

"Mrs. Hale is alone. She needs to know there are people in the community who are there for her."

It was *Miss* Hale. Carly's mom had never married, but George decided not to correct him. "There's nothing we can—"

"I spoke to my counselor on the way here. She's going to send me a list of grief services Carly's mom can access." He took a long drag on his cigarette.

"Why do you need me?" She hated that he was starting to make sense.

"You're on leave so you don't have anything better to do, and you knew Carly."

Damn. He made her feel selfish for shying away from a grieving mother.

George rubbed her temples, thinking. "We can't go without Liam's say-so." She unlocked her phone, opened her contact list, and passed it to him. "Enter your number. I'll call Liam, get the okay, and then I'll meet you there."

He tapped the screen and then stood. "Someone murdered

her."

"I know." She blinked back tears, her anguish overwhelming her.

He stood and walked past her, heading toward his truck. "The Solomon Islands are littered with unexploded ordnance from World War Two. People, children, are killed by accidental explosions. Dealing with death never gets any easier," he called over his shoulder.

"Maybe it's not supposed to." She waved goodbye and then went inside to call Liam.

CHAPTER FIVE

Randy climbed out of the truck as George wrapped her bike lock around a fence post in front of Susan Hale's house. He looked better than he had yesterday. He wore a lightweight gray winter jacket and a pair of jeans. His limp was hardly noticeable. Although he was still scruffy, he'd taken the time to comb his hair and shave.

She'd ridden her bike on the ice-covered trail to the home on Lakeshore Drive, which stood at the edge of town at the point where the paved road turned into a dirt track. Her fingers frozen, she fumbled as she unclipped her bike helmet. She tugged off her red fine-knit toque. She sported a black sweater and straight black pants under her navy down-filled coat.

Liam had worked late into the night. Not only had he helped the RCMP with their investigation, but he also performed his duties as police chief. His job involved an inordinate amount of paperwork, which would have driven her nuts, but he didn't seem to mind.

By the time he got home, he'd been exhausted, not just physically. Carly had been officially identified, and Susan Hale had been notified. He had been sparse with the details. She hadn't expected anything else. Having to inform a mother that her daughter was dead had taken an emotional toll on him.

He seemed to like the idea of her visiting Susan Hale and had even echoed Randy's argument that Carly's mom was alone and needed support. He would've objected if he had any suspicion that Randy was involved with Carly's death.

Randy approached, carrying a rectangular foil dish in one hand and a paper bag in the other. He passed the bag to her. "Here's Liam's clothes."

"Thanks." She stuffed them in the bike's saddle bags along with her helmet and hat.

"Nice day." He squinted up at the afternoon sun.

"What's that?" She pointed at the foil.

"It's a lasagna. You're supposed to bring food to the bereaved." His tone held a note of criticism.

"Of course." She put a hand to her head. It was a social convention, one that she'd forgotten.

"Don't worry about it. Luckily for you, I remembered." He turned and walked up the path.

Susan Hale's house was a small one-story home. Judging by the square shape of the building, George guessed it held a living room, one bathroom, a small kitchen, and probably one bedroom on the main floor. Any extra living space would be in the basement.

The door was answered by a large gray-haired woman wearing a pair of pale jeans and a skin-tight sweatshirt stretched over a large bust. "Hi, I'm Jan, a friend of Susan's."

"Hi, Jan, I'm George, and this is Randy. We knew Carly." Talking about Carly in the past tense felt wrong.

Without a word, Randy stepped forward and placed the lasagna in Jan's hands. "I brought this."

The stunned woman nodded, about-faced, and carried the dish to the kitchen, which was to the right of the entrance. It had brown dated linoleum flooring and a cream-colored fridge and stove. A white table with matching chairs sat in the center of the room.

Randy followed Jan inside. George hesitated, fighting the impulse to turn and walk away. It was too soon and felt like she was intruding on a mother's grief. But then George straightened her shoulders, gathered her courage, and entered.

Randy made his way along a short hallway to a cozy living room, which was painted a light coffee color. A picture window looked out over a small, treed garden. Susan Hale, Carly's mom, sat on a beige loveseat with photo albums scattered around her. Her eyes were red and puffy, and her nose swollen. A box of tissues sat on the coffee table in front of her. A pile of crumpled, used tissues littered the carpeted floor.

Randy cleared his throat and then said, "I know there's nothing I can say that'll make a difference, but I want you to know I'm here for you."

Susan looked up at him. "Were you a friend of Carly's?"

He shook his head. "I knew her, but not well. George here"—he pointed at her with his thumb—"was better acquainted."

She nodded solemnly. "I'm so sorry to intrude at this time. Carly and I talked a lot about school and her future."

Jan entered the living room carrying a mug of coffee in each hand. She shoved one cup at Randy, who grabbed it with both hands to prevent the liquid sloshing over the sides. George grasped the other mug before Jan could throw it at her. She ignored Jan's unfortunate manner. This wasn't the time or place to take offense.

Susan gave George a weak smile. "I remember. You said you'd go with her to the university and show her around."

"That's right." George had offered to help Carly get settled. Even though Edmonton wasn't large as cities went, it might seem overwhelming to a young woman from Magpie. Carly had rejected her help, wanting to explore with a friend from high school instead.

Susan stared out at the garden, lost in her thoughts, and then said, "I can't, for the life of me, understand what she was doing here in Magpie. She was supposed to be at the university, staying at the dorm. She wasn't due back until the beginning of December. That's when her term ends."

"And she didn't call during the school year?" George regretted the words as soon as she uttered them. She'd asked out of curiosity, but her question could easily be interpreted as disapproval.

Randy shot her a stern look.

"Carly said she was busy with projects." A tear trickled down Susan's cheek. "I assumed she would call if she got the chance. I phoned last week and left her a message. I just thought she was busy." Susan shook her head slightly, as though she couldn't quite believe this was happening.

"The police will probably want to know about her friends and boyfriends. You should prepare yourself for that." George gentled her tone.

"She hasn't mentioned anyone for ages, but I assumed she had someone. She had that sparkle in her eyes. You know the one. You have it when you look at that man of yours. When she was home for the summer, she'd finish work and then stay out all night. She would never tell me where she got to or who she was with. When I asked her, she'd just smile and change the subject."

"You didn't push?" George didn't really understand what a good mother-daughter relationship was like. Her own mom suffered from mental illness and didn't have the ability to care for her children.

Susan lifted her hands up and then let them fall into her lap. "Maybe I should have, but she was twenty-two. She was out on her own, an adult. Did you tell your mom where you were when you were that age? Truth is, she was just like me. Bad taste in men."

"And you're sure she had a man?" If Carly were seeing someone in Magpie, it would explain her presence in the area.

"Oh, yes." Susan gave George a sad smile, then her gaze focused on a framed photo of a little girl laughing. She pointed to the picture. "Look at her. That was taken when she was three. She would line up her dolls and teach them. Even at that age, she knew what she wanted to do." A sob erupted from her throat. "They'll never find who did it. They won't look that hard. If she was the daughter of a wealthy family, they might."

George crouched down in front of her. "I'm sure Liam will—"

"No, she's the illegitimate child of a cleaner." Susan grabbed George's hand. "You need to look into it for me."

"Me?" George couldn't contain her surprise. "I can't. I'm on sick leave. No one's going to share information with me. Besides, the RCMP are in charge of the investigation."

Susan tightened her grip; her fingers were ice-cold. "You figured out who robbed that armored truck and who killed that journalist. You can do the same for my girl."

Carly had been a shining light, someone who made the world a better place. George's heart hurt for Susan Hale. If agreeing to look into Carly's death gave her some comfort, then how could she say no? "I'll try. I can't promise anything, but I can try."

Susan nodded. "That's more than most will do."

George stood, needing to put some distance between herself and the grieving mother. She was uncomfortable with her promise, not because she didn't want to find out who'd killed Carly, but because she wasn't sure how she would keep it.

Randy pulled a piece of paper from his pocket and placed it on the coffee table. "This is the number of someone you can talk to, and I've added my number. When you're ready."

Susan blinked at him, seeming to see him for the first time. "Why are you helping me?"

He tapped his prosthetic leg. "It's been pointed out to me by my therapist that helping others is better than wallowing in self-pity."

He made a good point. He was a man who'd lost his leg, clearing unexploded bombs. Susan Hale had just lost her only child. George was all out of shape because she had epilepsy, had lost her job, and couldn't drive. Perhaps she should follow Randy's lead and stop feeling sorry for herself. Someone had killed a sweet young woman who had so much to offer the world. If she could help find Carly's killer, she would.

They said their goodbyes and left, heading out as the late afternoon sun was sinking low on the western horizon.

She hunched her shoulders against the cold. "Will you be okay?" she asked Randy as he headed for his truck.

He opened the door but hesitated. After a moment, he said, "Yeah, I'll call a buddy, and I have an appointment with my therapist tomorrow. Don't worry about me. Help Ms. Hale find closure."

"I'll do what I can."

CHAPTER SIX

George decided to walk her bike across the highway to the Charm Hotel. Normally, she'd go to the Jumping Bean coffee shop, but she didn't want to talk to the owner, her friend Olivia. George wasn't good at hiding her feelings, and Olivia was bound to notice her emotional state.

She stopped at a house two doors down from Susan Hale's with a *For Sale* sign in the front lawn. It was about fifty years old but had a good view of the lake and a treed yard. The property had always been known as the Osbourne House after the family that built it. The siding was an ugly yellow color, but the location was amazing.

She turned right at the sports center and then took a left onto Main Street. Unfortunately, she didn't have any savings, and there was no way she would qualify for a mortgage. She pushed her bike over a rut in the road. There was no point in wanting something that could never be. She passed the grocery store and headed towards the highway. She needed to stop daydreaming and focus on helping Carly's mom.

She dodged the busy traffic on the highway and reached the Charm Hotel in less than fifteen minutes. It was a three-story building, which boasted a four-star rating. It housed a fancy restaurant and a decent coffee shop. It wouldn't hurt to have a coffee. People would've heard about Carly's death by now, and her colleagues might want to share their stories about her. George had nothing better to do with her time than sit and listen.

She locked her bike in the rack near the main entrance and then texted Liam to let him know where she was. With any luck, he would finish work soon and she could get a ride home.

The trip to town from her house had been rough. She'd skidded twice on her skinny tires. If she was going to cycle through the ice and snow, she needed studded winter tires. She'd seen some on the internet. They were about the same price as the ones for her car. Why would she go to that expense for a bike she didn't own? Once she was home, she'd call Buddy to come and pick it up. Maybe she'd buy one next summer, or once she was seizure-free for six months, she could get her license back. The latter was an option she hadn't allowed herself to consider until now, mainly because she wasn't sure how comfortable she would be behind the wheel. What if she had an epileptic episode while driving and killed someone? How would she live with that?

She made her way through the hotel's reception area. Her visit with Susan Hale had been unnerving.

She ordered a latte and headed for a spot by the window where she could watch the traffic on the highway. She tried to distract herself by thinking about what kind of job she could do once her sick leave ran out. Even if she were able to drive again, she wouldn't be able to work in law enforcement.

She pictured Carly's smiling face. Her vision blurred as tears filled her eyes. Using the back of her hand, she wiped them away. The shock of Carly's death hit her all over again. Why would someone kill such a dear, sweet, young woman? Maybe it hadn't been intentional, only an accident, and the culprit had panicked and dumped the body.

George took out her phone and searched for Carly's social media accounts. Once she located them, she scrolled through. There were pictures from her classes at school, but they were all group photos. No one caught George's eye.

"Excuse me." A young woman who couldn't be more than sixteen stood in front of her. She wore her black curly hair in pigtails. Her dark eyes were red-rimmed, a sign she'd been crying.

"Hi." George had been so caught up in her thoughts she didn't see the young woman approach.

"Did you know Carly? I thought I saw you talking to her a while ago." The girl wore a burgundy vest over her jeans and T-shirt, which told George she was one of the hotel's housekeeping staff.

"Yes. I'm George." She pointed to the chair opposite. "Please join me."

"Cindy." She tapped her chest as she took the offered seat. "We're not supposed to sit in here, but-but..." Cindy blinked, fighting back tears.

George gave her a moment to regain her composure and then said, "Are you in high school?"

Cindy nodded.

"Its mid-afternoon. Shouldn't you be in class?"

"I have a free period every other day, so I come in and do laundry. I also work weekends. It's good. I don't have to work evenings and nights, so I have lots of time for homework."

"That was the kind of thing Carly would do," George said. "How well did you know her?"

"We worked together last summer. I haven't seen her since." Cindy pulled a tissue from her pocket and dabbed her eyes.

"Not even around town?"

"No."

"You don't know if she had a boyfriend?" George knew she was pushing the young woman in her obvious grief, but she'd made a promise, and if she was going to keep it, she had to figure out if Carly had a love interest.

Cindy stared out of the window. "She was seeing someone, but it was hush-hush."

"Why was it hush-hush?" George asked, repeating the term.

"Because he was married."

George leaned back in her seat. That would explain the secrecy. "Did she tell you her boyfriend was married?"

"Yes. We were cleaning one of the larger suites. It's a big job. We do that in teams. She said she never thought she'd fall for a married man."

"Did you ask who it was?" George touched her coffee mug. It was cold. She didn't take a sip.

"Yes, but she would never say." Cindy tugged a napkin from the ornate metal dispenser on the table and blew her nose again.

"Who else did she hang out with in town? She must've had other friends." George wished she'd brought her notebook.

"Not that I could tell. She was a hard worker, though. She was always studying something."

Carly was quiet, kind, and always had her nose in a book. George softened her tone. "That's how I remember her, too."

"I try to follow her example." Cindy extracted a copy of *King Lear* from her pocket and gave George a watery smile. "We have to read it for school, so I try and make the most of my breaks."

"That's good." It was a weak response, but it was the best George could do.

"I should go. I have another load of sheets to put in the wash." Cindy sniffed as she stood and walked across the lobby. She then turned left, heading down the hallway out of sight.

George switched her gaze back to the passing traffic, allowing the events of the day to roll over her. Most murders were committed by the people closest to the victim. She dismissed the idea that a relative could have killed Carly. As far as she knew, the only close family Carly had was her mother. But Cindy was the second person to suggest that Carly had a man in her life, a secret boyfriend, a married man. Something like that festered, and it rarely ended well.

CHAPTER SEVEN

Liam snagged a beer out of the fridge. He'd been too exhausted to talk on the drive home. Not that it had mattered because Georgina had been lost in her thoughts. It didn't take a genius to know she was thinking about Carly. Georgina didn't deal well with death. Thankfully, she had no idea how the young woman had been killed. Randy knew how Carly had died. The world-weary soldier had probably seen more than his fair share of bodies.

Someone beat her to death, didn't they? Randy had made that observation when Liam had questioned him at the crime scene. Liam had sworn him to secrecy, explaining that Carly's mother didn't need to hear it as gossip. He had agreed.

Liam leaned against the counter, twisted the top off his bottle of beer, and took a long swallow. Georgina eyed Liam as she entered the kitchen, her long dark hair wet from her shower. Her changeable eyes looked green in the artificial light.

"I'd ask if you had a bad day, but I already know the answer." She put her arms around his waist and held him.

He reciprocated, rubbing her back through her robe. Her face was still red from cycling all the way into town through the snow and ice on a bike with no snow tires. She'd left the bicycle at the Charm Hotel and walked to the police station to meet him. She'd finally decided to do the sensible thing and give it back to Buddy. Normally, he'd tease her about it, but now wasn't the time. "I called Buddy when you were in the shower. We don't need to bring the bike back here. He said he'll pick it up at the hotel."

"Thanks," she murmured against his chest, still holding him tight.

They needed to move, but she kept stalling. A small part of him wondered if it was because she was having second thoughts about living with him. But his common sense told him that if she wanted him gone, she would've kicked his butt out already. No, there was something else preventing her from making a commitment. They needed to talk it out, but he wasn't going to approach the subject this evening because he didn't have the energy.

She moved out of his embrace and checked the timer on the stove.

He downed another mouthful of beer. He didn't drink often, mainly because Georgina wasn't a drinker and imbibing alone wasn't his thing.

"I was in the mood for lasagna because Randy gave one to Susan Hale. It will be ready in a couple of minutes." She poured herself a decaf coffee from the pot on the counter. "You might need a second bottle."

He straightened as the hairs on the back of his neck stood on end. "What happened?"

If she was suggesting he have a second beer, then something was wrong. As the daughter of a drug dealer, the most addictive substance she consumed was caffeine.

She bit her lip. "I made a promise, and I don't know if I can keep it."

"To whom?"

"Susan Hale."

"The victim's mother?" Too late he realised that giving her permission to visit Susan Hale was probably a mistake. "What did you promise her?"

"She begged me to look into Carly's death." She rubbed her hands down her robe, a nervous reaction.

"You're kidding. You're not a cop. I guess technically, you still are. But you're a community police officer." Although, that hadn't stopped her solving crimes this past summer.

She plopped down at the kitchen table. "You're right, and I know it's none of my business."

He remembered how she'd interacted with Carly. Georgina had acted as a mentor, trying to help the younger woman. It was only natural that she would want to know who killed her. "But she was your friend."

Georgina rubbed her temples as though the action would help her organize her thoughts. "It's more than that. I watched out for her when she was a teen because I related to her. Magpie is a town where there are a lot of middle-class church-going people, but Carly and I weren't part of that group. I, as you know, am the daughter of a criminal, and she was the child of a single parent. People looked down on us."

"You were both outsiders." He crossed the room and joined her, taking a seat at the table, placing his beer bottle in front of him.

"Yes, and Susan Hale believes that no one will look into Carly's death because she's the child of a cleaning lady." She placed her hand over his. "I don't believe that, but at the same time—"

"You have to do what you can." One of the reasons she'd made such a good community officer was because she empathized with people. He turned his palm up, wrapping his fingers around hers.

"Does that make sense to you?"

"It does." He'd grown up in an upper middle-class family and had been given the benefit of the doubt when it came to his teen pranks, but not everyone was that lucky, and labels stuck.

Georgina had worked all her adult life to overcome her father's crimes. Hank Scott had abused his wife and daughters. She'd defied him at every turn. Carly's story was different, but Georgina and Carly had both been born on the proverbial wrong side of the tracks.

If Georgina didn't investigate, it would eat at her. He was the Magpie Police Chief, and although a homicide investigation fell under the jurisdiction of the RCMP, he would be given some latitude. "I'll help on one condition. We give whatever information we find to Mia."

She gave him a dazzling smile that justified all the complaints he'd get from his former boss.

She took a sip of her coffee. "You should tell her that Carly's mother and a colleague at the Charm Hotel both thought she had a mysterious boyfriend."

"Mysterious boyfriend?" How long had she been on the case, a couple of hours? "You already have a lead?"

She shrugged. "I wouldn't exactly call it a lead. It's more of a hint."

"But still, that's fast."

"People tell me things. Oh, and before I forget, the friend, a teen named Cindy, thought he was married. Mia will probably want to question them both."

The timer buzzed, telling them the lasagna was ready. She rose, grabbed her oven gloves from where they lay on the kitchen counter, and then pulled the foil pan out of the oven.

He took another sip of his beer, stood, and then started laying the table. "The best thing we can do is figure out who her friends were. Someone will know something."

"Agreed. Where do you want to start?" She walked to the fridge, grabbed a bag of prepared salad, ripped it open, and dumped it into a bowl.

It felt right to be working a case with Georgina again. "Let's eat and then get an early night. We'll drive to the university in the morning and talk to her friends."

CHAPTER EIGHT

George put on her sunglasses to protect her eyes from the rising sun as they negotiated the Edmonton city streets near the University of Alberta. The two-hour drive from Magpie felt like a vacation. She hadn't realized how much she needed a break from her regular routine and how much she'd missed being able to just get in her car and go. They'd left early, hoping to get there while Carly's friends and acquaintances were still at the dorms and hadn't yet left for their classes.

Liam had cleared their inquiry with Mia and confirmed that the crime scene techs had already gone over Carly's dorm room and taken what little evidence they could find.

Three magpies swooped down to peck at a discarded fast-food wrapper that sat on the sidewalk.

"Three for a girl," George whispered.

"What did you say?"

"It's nothing." She waved a dismissive hand.

"Tell me."

"There's this old English superstition about magpies. If you only see one, then that's for sorrow. Two is for joy."

"And three for a girl." He repeated her words.

"You did hear me. When I was young, my mom believed the magpie rhyme was true. Which was a pain because there are magpies everywhere. She'd see one, think it was a bad omen, and then go back to bed for the day. There was this one time when she saw six of them. She packed up all her things, convinced she would soon have enough money to get away."

"Why? What does six magpies mean?"

"Six is for gold."

Her mom had sat in their dirty living room all day with her belongings piled around her. What had hurt George the most wasn't her mom's mental illness; it was the fact that she hadn't planned to take her daughters with her.

"That's a lot for a kid to deal with." He placed his hand over hers for a moment, offering her his support.

The morning sun sparkled on the water as the highway crossed the North Saskatchewan River. George's childhood was such a long time ago. She'd been helpless back then, tossed between the whims of her drug dealer father and her mentally ill mother. Now she was a strong, confident woman, and yet she could never completely dismiss her past. It was a part of her, which was something she didn't want to think about right now.

George stuffed her travel mug into the cup holder. "You know, when I was at university, I never went to visit Grace. She always came and stayed with me here in Edmonton."

Liam had worn his uniform, and they'd driven one of the Magpie Police Service SUVs for the trip. He claimed people were more likely to answer questions if he looked like a cop and didn't roll up in a ten-year-old beat-up Subaru. He had a point.

"Did you live on campus?" He looked cool, sexy, and lethal with his sunglasses, short-cropped hair, and bent nose.

"At first, but I was living off student loans so it was just cheaper to rent an apartment. I wasn't into the campus life anyway." She'd also worked at a local burger joint to earn some extra money.

"No sororities or wild parties for you?" Liam drove past the university hospital.

"No. Not my scene. Turn left at these lights and then left again at the next set. That'll take you into the dorm parking lot." The place had changed in small ways since her time here. The sidewalk had been widened. But the university still had the same energy, a feeling of hope for a brighter future.

"This place is much bigger than I expected," Liam stated as he reversed into a parking spot.

"There are over five hundred buildings. It's easy to get turned around." She had gotten lost nearly every day for the first month she was here.

He climbed out of the SUV and shrugged into his police-issue winter coat. He fished his notebook out of his pants pocket. "Mia has already called campus security and cleared us. She stayed in room thirty-five B."

They walked together through the parking lot. Liam stepped back allowing George to go first once they reached the building.

"That was nice of Mia." She flung the steel and glass entrance open

He led the way, taking the stairs to the second floor. He then followed the door numbers until they came to Carly's room. He passed her a pair of latex gloves. "Just in case."

She snapped them on as he opened the door.

The room was tiny. It just fit a bed and a corner desk. There was a small built-in closet at the foot of the bed to George's right. The walls were constructed of large cement blocks that were painted white. Every surface was covered with a thin layer of fingerprint dust, including the desk, the head and footboard, the windowsill, and every doorknob and handle.

"Where's her stuff?" Liam paced to the closet and peeked inside. "Nothing."

"Do you think the techs could have taken it?"

"No. Look at the dust. There are no dust-free places where a book might have been. There's nothing, and I'll bet there was nothing here when they arrived."

George peered under the bed. "Do you think she packed her things and left, or did someone else pack for her?"

"You mean after she died?" Liam slid open a desk drawer.

George shrugged. "Maybe."

She assessed the room. When Carly had first moved into the residence, George had advised her to always hide her personal documents. *Never under the mattress. Everyone looks there. Make it somewhere that doesn't catch the eye.* "If Carly had any valuables, where would she have hidden them?"

"I always like the air conditioning vents." He pointed to the opening in the ceiling.

"Carly was short. Even with a chair, she'd have a hard time reaching that." She scanned the room. "I wouldn't put anything behind the curtains. Maybe between the bed and the wall."

Liam put a hand under the footboard and gave it an experimental tug. "That's heavy. I don't see her being able to budge it. And if Carly hid her stuff, she would need to be able to retrieve it."

It only took her two steps to cross the room. "I taught Carly that the dorm is essentially a long-term hotel full of students. There's always a bad apple." George blinked back tears as the memory and her emotions threatened to overwhelm her control.

Liam put an arm around her shoulders. "What kind of things would she have hidden?"

"Her papers." She looked up at him. "You know, her birth certificate, social insurance card, and passport, if she had one. Basically, the stuff people use to steal your identity." There were two cubbies on the left side of the desk, a single draw on the right, and a gap in the middle for a seat. She got on her hands and knees and crawled underneath.

"Hah! There it is, behind the draw." She yanked out a sealed plastic bag with some cash, a birth certificate, a plastic card with her social insurance number, and a phone. She backed out and passed it to him. "Here."

"I wasn't expecting her phone to be in it." Liam opened it and retrieved the smartphone.

She stood next to him, peering over his shoulder. "That bag raises a lot of questions, but it answers one."

"She didn't pack the room herself. I wonder where her stuff went." He pressed the home button, but the screen was blank, indicating the phone was out of charge.

"Storage or a dump would be my guess." She hated the idea of someone throwing away Carly's stuff. "Do you think that's Carly's only phone, or do you think she had a second one?"

He stuffed the device back in the plastic bag. "There had to be a second phone, probably for the married boyfriend, if he exists."

"Or this could be her second phone and she had her regular one on her. One thing's for sure, no young woman would go anywhere without her phone." George wished she'd known about the married boyfriend and had somehow been able to protect Carly. But that wasn't how things worked. She couldn't stop anyone from making their own decisions, even if they were bad ones.

"I'll call Mia. She'll want this." He waved the bag.

George walked to the window, which looked out over another wing of the residence. "You know what bothers me?"

"You're going to tell me."

"Why did Carly keep coming back to Magpie? Yes, her mom was there, but wouldn't she just come back for a visit? Plus, Susan could have visited her here. But this past summer, she headed back. There are much better job opportunities in Edmonton. Why work part-time at the Rockin Horse and then later at the hotel? Something drew her back."

"Yeah, but it might not be that mysterious. She might have just been homesick. It does happen. Not everyone is cut out for city life." He took out his phone and dialed. "Hi, Mia, it's Liam. We found something you're going to want to see. Call me back when you get this message."

CHAPTER NINE

"What now?" George scanned the long hallway as she closed the door to Carly's dorm room. The brown vinyl floors and painted block walls reminded her of her first year here. It was a time in her life when she thought anything was possible. Not once did it occur to her that she'd end up back in Magpie.

"We should talk to the other students." Liam knocked on the door opposite. "Carly might have been more forthcoming with people who don't live in Magpie."

They heard movement on the other side of the door, but no one answered.

Liam knocked again. "This is the police. I'd like to talk to you about Carly Hale."

A slim woman with burgundy hair swung open the door. "What about her?" Her lip curled in a sneer at the sight of Liam in his police uniform.

"Do you know she's dead?" It wasn't George's job to inform her of Carly's death, but it was obvious the young woman didn't like cops. If she knew the importance of their questions, she might be more helpful.

The young woman gasped as her dark eyes widened. "No, that can't be true."

"I'm afraid it is." Liam softened his tone. "When did you last see her?"

She put a hand to her mouth as a tear leaked from the corner of her eye. "A couple of weeks ago. How was she killed? What happened to her?"

"It's best not to talk about it," Liam said tactfully. "You want to remember her the way she was."

She gasped. "Oh, no. This must be a mistake."

"What's your name?" George asked.

"Jackie Jones. My parents have a thing about alliteration." It was a rehearsed response, one she had probably said countless times.

"Did Carly have any trouble with anyone? Was there anyone she didn't get along with?" Liam pulled out his notebook.

Jackie's lips trembled. "No, everyone liked her."

"Did she socialize with you?" Liam's tone was even, showing no emotion.

"No, but she did a few projects with my boyfriend. He's an art major. They had some courses together." Her voice shook.

"You never saw her at parties or hung out together?" Liam pushed.

"No. She kept to herself. There was one incident about a month ago." Her eyes narrowed, and she poked the air with her index finger. "An older woman showed up. She was screaming and banging on the door, calling Carly a bitch and home-wrecker."

"A home-wrecker?" Liam scribbled the answer in his book. "That's a very specific accusation. Did you ever see her with a man?"

Jackie shook her head, making her burgundy hair fall about her face. "No, and Carly didn't seem the type who'd be stupid enough to go out with a married man. Especially when there were plenty of single guys who would have been interested, but I guess you never know."

"And this woman definitely called her a home-wrecker. Are you sure about that?" Liam asked, confirming her answer.

"Oh, yes, I was studying for a midterm, and the noise was distracting."

"How did Carly react?"

Jackie gulped in a breath, obviously feeling the shock of Carly's death. "She didn't open her door."

"Did you get a look at Carly's accuser?" Liam followed his line of questioning, making Jackie remember the incident.

"I did." Jackie nodded. "Although I didn't talk to her either. I didn't want her to turn her anger on me. She looked ready to tear someone apart."

"Can you describe her?"

Jackie closed her eyes, recalling the moment. "She was slim with blond hair, and she looked rich."

"How does someone look rich?" Liam's eyebrows drew together in question.

George cut her gaze to him. Even she knew that people looked rich because they wore expensive clothing.

Jackie put a finger to her lips as she thought about her answer. Her nails were painted with chipped black polish. "Her coat and her purse. She had a fancy purse with chrome buckles and stuff. And her black coat looked like it cost over a thousand bucks."

George inwardly groaned at her own stupidity. Liam was forcing Jackie to remember the details and not the generalizations.

"What color was her hair?" Liam continued.

Jackie's eyes narrowed. "I already said she was blond, but she wasn't a natural one. She had different shades in her hair. It was very well done, and she had the kind of flawless skin rich people have. It makes you think they have a facial every day." She held her hands in the air, palms up. "That's all I know."

Liam passed her his card. "If you think of anything else, give me a call."

"Are you going to be okay? Is there someone you can call?" George asked. It didn't seem as though Jackie had been a close friend of Carly's, but she'd received a shock, nonetheless.

Jackie gave George a sad smile. "Thanks. I'll call my boyfriend."

"Maybe you should make an appointment with one of the counselors on campus," Liam advised.

They said their goodbyes and then knocked on a few other dorm rooms, but no one could tell them anything about Carly except that she was nice and kept to herself. And no one else had witnessed the woman banging on Carly's door.

Liam called Mia again as they climbed in the car. "Where are you? I want to hand off a plastic bag we found with Carly Hale's papers and phone. And there's a witness you should probably talk to, a Jackie Jones."

She could hear Mia's raised voice even though the phone wasn't on speaker. It stood to reason that she was pissed. They had removed evidence from a potential crime scene, but they'd been in a difficult situation. Once they discovered it, they couldn't leave it unguarded.

"I'll drop it over to you on my way out of town." Liam hung up and stuffed his phone in his pocket.

"She has no right to be mad at us. She gave us permission to visit the dorm room. Besides, the crime scene techs should have found it yesterday." George readied her defense in case Mia decided to blast her with her infamous temper.

"I'll tell her that when I drop the bag off at Division K headquarters." He pressed the start button to turn on the engine.

The RCMP, being a Canada-wide police service, was divided into fourteen divisions. Each province or territory had their own division, and Ottawa, the capital, had a separate one for their special duties. Alberta was designated Division K.

"Before we head that way, can we make a quick stop at the Fine Arts Building? I need to see something."

He turned to her, his brow wrinkling. "What's that?"

"Her art."

CHAPTER TEN

The gray stone frontage to the Fine Arts Building looked plain and drab, which was a surprise. Liam had expected some type of art deco architecture with weird lines, but the building seemed surprisingly conventional. "What do you hope to find here?"

"I told you, her art." Georgina gave him a look that suggested the answer was obvious.

"Why?" He was missing something.

"I'm not artistic in any way, but I've been told that people express themselves through their creations." Georgina pulled on the brass door handle and entered the building.

He followed behind her. "And you think Carly might have put something into her paintings that will tell us who this mystery man was?"

"I don't know." She scrunched her face, making her small nose crinkle. "She wanted to be a teacher, so she might have been taking courses that complement her chosen profession. When I used to give my drug talks at the school, the walls were always covered in drawings. Kids seem to like that kind of stuff."

They strolled through the hallways, scanning the art for signatures. As far as Liam was concerned, this was a colossal waste of time, but he'd let Georgina go with her hunch for a while longer.

"Look." She was six feet behind him. She threw her backpack on the ground and snagged her phone from the front pouch.

"What is it?" He rushed to her side. A mishmash of photos surrounded a sketch of a naked couple embracing. Each snapshot depicted another couple. All of them represented some degree of intimacy, whether it was holding hands, kissing, or sex.

"That's Carly." She pointed to an image on the right side of the collage. Carly was laughing as a man placed a morsel of food in her mouth. His face was in profile, making it difficult to identify him.

Georgina stretched taller in an effort to get closer to the image. Using her smartphone, she took shots of Carly and her boyfriend and then stepped back, taking a picture of the art as a whole. "I think I know this guy." She squinted at her phone screen.

"Who is it?" Liam peered over her shoulder. He was pleased he'd let Georgina follow her hunch. He never would have thought to look at Carly's art, and he wasn't sure Mia would have thought of it either. That was the difference between how he handled a criminal investigation and Georgina's more holistic approach. She looked at the whole person, whereas he followed the evidence. Maybe it was her personal connection to Carly Hale that gave her insight. If there was a lesson to be learned from this moment, it was that he needed to trust her intuition.

"I can't be sure because of the angle, but I think his name is Nathan Wells. He owns Wells Automotive. Actually, he inherited it from his father a few years ago."

Liam had heard the name. It was the only garage in Magpie. He had never talked to Nathan Wells or used his garage. He got Buddy, Georgina's life-long friend, to service their Subaru. "What do you know about him?"

"Not much." She stuffed her phone back in her bag. "I'm a small fry, and he's a big fish. If he had a problem, he would've gone to Chief Hunt and then later Chief Evans. Nathan Wells wouldn't deal with an underling like me."

"We'll get Mia's people to scour Carly's art. I have to get back to work." The discovery of Carly's body had interrupted his meeting with the mayor and the town council. It had been rescheduled for this afternoon, and it would take two hours to drive back to Magpie. But before they left town, they had to stop at RCMP Division K.

****

George waited in the car while Liam went into the orange

41

brick building to talk to Mia. It was now obvious that the rumours were true: Carly had been seeing a married man. Why would a young, beautiful woman who had her whole life ahead of her settle for a man who was a cheater? George opened the photo album on her phone and stared at the picture that had been part of the art display. She seemed so vivacious and alive. Maybe the answer was that simple. This man had made her happy.

But married men rarely left their wives. What would George have done if Liam had been already married when she'd met him? He could have been, and she would never have known. He'd been investigating her then, pretending to be her new work partner, and going by the name of Liam Mackie. She'd fallen for him hard. It was only by pure luck that he'd felt the same about her and had decided to stay in Magpie.

Her phone buzzed, and Olivia's number appeared on the screen.

"Hi," she answered, happy to hear from her friend.

Olivia groaned.

George was instantly alert. "What's wrong?"

"Damn old age."

"What happened?" George guessed Olivia to be in her sixties, although she had the energy of a teen.

"I slid on the ice and broke my ankle." Her pain was apparent in her strangled tone.

"What can I do?"

"I'm fine. I'm at the hospital, and John's here looking after me, but I was wondering…" Olivia hesitated, obviously not wanting to ask a big favor.

"What is it?" George tried to rein in her usual impatience. Olivia was hurt and probably feeling a little vulnerable.

"Would you mind covering at the Jumping Bean? Mel, who delivers my baked goods, is covering for now. She's probably rushed off her feet. She has to pick her kids up from school by three. She'll just have to leave if I don't have a replacement."

"No problem. I'm happy to help out, but I'm in Edmonton. It'll take me a couple of hours to get there."

"I knew you'd help."

George could hear the relief in Olivia's voice. "Did you just get to the hospital?"

"Yes, I've had the X-rays. I'm just waiting to get my cast."

"I've been told a walking cast is best. If it can be done with your injury."

"What's a walking cast?"

"It's a cast that allows you to hobble about. When Smokey broke his leg, the crutches hurt more than the break because they rubbed his underarms raw. Talk to Dr. Sullivan. She'll tell you what's what."

She could hear a murmuring in the background, and then Olivia said, "John knows what you're talking about. I'll text Mel and tell her you'll be there as soon as you can."

"You got it."

Liam climbed back in the car just as she was hanging up. "What's going on?"

"Olivia broke her ankle. I'm going to help out at the coffee shop. Was Mia pissed?" she asked, changing the subject.

He pressed the start button and reversed out of the parking spot. "Yes. She's raving mad. I've never seen her so livid."

"But she gave us permission to go there," she said, repeating her earlier argument.

He turned onto the highway heading west. "She's not pissed at us. The crime scene techs should have found it. Up until now, they've been working on the theory that Carly packed up and left.

"There's no way she would've quit school. She wanted to be a teacher for as long as I can remember. Her mom said as much yesterday. And she never would have left behind her personal documents."

"Exactly." He checked the rearview mirror, looked over his shoulder, and then switched into the fast lane. "And now that they have proof she didn't pack her room herself, they have to consider that someone, or maybe multiple someones, packed up her stuff after they killed her. It's changed the direction of the case."

"There was no point in continuing that line of inquiry if it was wrong. And that's not our fault."

He placed his hand over hers. "No, it's not. You showed them up, that's all. Mia will get over it."

She laced her fingers through his. "What did Mia say about Nathan Wells?"

"She was tight-lipped. I don't know if they knew about him or not. But she did say not to approach him. She'd look into it."

"Good." The RCMP were on the case. She could relax and focus on Olivia. It didn't matter who caught Carly's killer as long as they were brought to justice.

CHAPTER ELEVEN

Liam stared at the mountain of files on his desk. He turned on his computer. The badge over his email app told him that there were over two hundred messages in his inbox. *Damn.*

Despite the reports and paperwork, he didn't miss working undercover with the RCMP. The position of police chief was challenging in different ways, and he'd been ready for the change. Mia had suggested that this role was his way of taking a sabbatical. She was wrong. This was the first time he had a home since he'd left university fifteen years ago. He worked with a great team, he was part of a community, and he woke up each day next to a beautiful, intelligent woman who kept him on his toes.

Helping out at the Jumping Bean would probably keep Georgina out of trouble for a few hours. He'd seen the devastation in her eyes when she'd talked about Carly's death. It was personal for her. He understood why she'd made a promise to Susan Hale, but she'd plunged them into a delicate situation. She couldn't interfere with the case. If she did, she would be charged.

His phone rang. The piercing tone told him that Mia was on the line.

"Carly was dead when she went into the lake." Mia hadn't bothered with small talk, which Liam appreciated given how busy he was.

He grabbed a pen and scribbled the information on his notepad. "Do they have a time of death?"

"The ME thinks she was there between ten days and two weeks."

That meant the trail was already cold. "Was she dumped where she was found, or did she drift?"

"The ME and crime scene techs are talking to a specialist in Charm Lake currents, but the initial answer is that she didn't drift. Someone weighted her down with sandbags, which they secured with nylon rope."

He closed his eyes, remembering the yellow coil around her waist. "And the rope came loose."

"Yes, that and the natural decomposition process bloated the body."

"Making her float." He stared at his notes and then said, "So someone tied her up, weighted her with sandbags, and threw her in—"

"Yes." Mia hung up as abruptly as she'd started their conversation. He was surprised she'd called at all. Maybe it was just a professional courtesy.

CHAPTER TWELVE

George arrived at the Jumping Bean coffee shop to find the place in chaos. Customers were lined up out the door. There were dirty coffee cups and plates piled high on every table.

Melissa Anderson, who everyone called Mel, snapped at the older woman standing in front of her. "Do I look like I have time to clean tables?"

Mel was probably in her early forties but had the under-eye bags and gaunt features of someone ten years older. Her hair was covered by a ball cap, and she wore a torn T-shirt and a pair of sweatpants. She was a wonderful baker. Her rich, moist brownies were the best George had ever tasted. But she had a brusque personality and was famous for speaking her mind. Her husband worked away in one of the northern mines. People cruelly joked that he'd chosen the job to get away from her.

George walked around the queue and made her way to Mel's side.

"What are you doing here? Get back. This is for staff only," Mel barked.

George held up her hands in a surrender motion. "Olivia said she'd contact you. She asked me to come and help."

"Oh, thank God." Mel's relief was obvious. "I haven't had a chance to look at my phone."

"Why don't you take a break? Maybe get a drink and something to eat," George suggested. "Then you can start clearing up while I serve the customers."

"The cranberry muffins are all there's left." She pointed to six muffins that were still in a rubber container instead of the glass display case. Poor Mel hadn't even had time to unpack them this morning.

"We can't sell what we don't have." George shrugged. "Let's just concentrate on getting the place in order so we can have a better day tomorrow."

"Will Olivia be back by then?"

"I don't know. She said her ankle is broken. I'll check on her tonight after work." *After work.* It'd been a long time since George had uttered those words. It felt good to be productive again. She smiled at the elderly woman who was next in line. "Give me a minute to get organized."

She poured some coffee into the grinder and set two pots to brew, one regular and the other decaf. Then she refilled the creamer station, making sure it was stocked.

People in the line were grumbling, but it would be faster in the long run if she didn't have to stop every time they ran out of something. Finally, she took her first customer's order.

Luckily, the sweet older woman just wanted a cup of tea. George grabbed a metal tea pot from the tray under the counter, added a teabag, filled it with hot water, and then placed it in front of her along with a cup. The next man just wanted a large black coffee. So far so good.

George worked her way through the line. Olivia's till was the old kind where you pressed down the keys, which forced George to do the math in her head in order to make change. No one had asked to pay with their debit cards, which George was dreading. Olivia had a system that worked with a tablet, but it was locked, and George didn't know the password.

"I can only take cash," she announced to everyone waiting.

"That's not right," grumbled a man she didn't recognize.

George simply shrugged. "I'm just helping out. The owner broke her ankle, and I can't get into the system."

There were more grumblings, but a customer said to the man next to him. "I can get yours. It's your turn next time."

A few negotiations were made as people figured out how to pay for their drinks.

"I'm back," Mel announced. It hadn't even been five minutes. "I'll do the dishes. Let's get everything clean before I have to take off."

"Can you sign me in to the debit system?"

"I can't get into it either. I've been turning people away all morning," Mel admitted.

George winced. Olivia was a savvy businesswoman. She wouldn't like hearing that. "Before you start, can you please put up a *cash only* sign out front. That way people won't have to wait if they can't pay."

"Right." Mel grabbed an eraser and a piece of chalk from a drawer and rushed outside to change the chalkboard.

Word had probably already spread around town, but there were always people who were out of the loop.

She spotted Elijah from the library in the lineup. "Hey, can you tell Mel to add *Olivia broke her ankle* to the board? So people know what's going on."

He gave her the thumbs up and went to talk to Mel.

Eventually, the line cleared. Mel had done a great job tidying the café. George set to work stocking the coffees, syrups, and other supplies needed to get the job done.

Buddy sat at a table near the window, talking with a young man who looked to be about Carly's age.

"Hey, Buddy, aren't you going to introduce me to your friend?" George called.

Buddy frowned. "Did you have a falling out with the police chief?"

She gave him a look that hopefully suggested he was crazy. "No. Why would you think that?"

He laughed and then said, "'Introduce me to your friend' is a pickup line."

"It is?" George blushed.

"Even I know that, and I've been married for fifteen years," Mel said as she was loading the dishwasher.

"Oh." Annoyed with herself for making such a blunder, she waved Buddy over.

"What?" he said as he joined her at the till.

"For the record, when I say things like that, it's never a pickup line," George snapped.

He grinned. "I know. That's what made it so funny."

49

"How well did you know Carly Hale?"

He shook his head. "Not at all."

George eyed the young man at Buddy's table. "Did your friend know her? He looks about the right age."

Mel stopped wiping down the work surfaces and moved to stand next to them, making it obvious that she was listening in.

George didn't want to tell her to leave. That would be rude. She figured she'd just have to be tactful. This was, after all, a public place.

"Hey, Noah." Buddy waved his friend over.

Noah joined them. He was tall and thin with dark hair. He had a sparsely stubbled chin, which suggested he was failing in his attempt to grow a beard.

"George, this is Noah Fournier. Noah, this is George Scott. She's an ex-cop who should be keeping her nose out of police business." Buddy's tone was flat and his face expressionless, making it obvious that he was unimpressed by her curiosity.

"It's not my idea," George admitted. "Susan Hale, Carly's mom, asked me to look into it."

Buddy sighed and then nodded. "How do you say no to that?" He turned to Noah. "Answer her questions."

"Noah, did you go to school with Carly?" George asked.

"She was a year younger than me but, yeah, I knew her." Noah made good eye contact. There was no sign that he was uncomfortable with her question.

"Did she still party with her friends here in Magpie?"

He shook his head. "Not really."

"Why not?" Maybe there had been a falling out.

Noah shrugged his skinny shoulders. He obviously didn't know, which was not a surprise. Sometimes people drifted apart as their lives took them in different directions.

"Was she well-liked?" George pressed.

"Oh, yeah, she used to tutor the younger kids. Everyone thought she was nice, but she wasn't the partying type." He glanced at Buddy and then looked down at his hands. "I hate that she's gone."

George knew how he felt. She patted his arm, giving him her silent support.

"Hey, George. What are you doing behind the counter?" Her sister, Grace, bounced onto a stool at the bar and pulled her long blond mane back from her face, revealing her perfect complexion, which was paler than usual today. She was the epitome of a girly-girl and had made her gift for doing hair and makeup into a multi-salon business.

"Olivia hurt her ankle. I'm helping." George waved a hand toward Buddy. "Grace, you know Buddy, and this is his friend Noah."

Noah smiled and blushed while Buddy simply nodded. "How're you doing?" He didn't look at Grace when he spoke to her, which struck George as off.

Mel tapped her on the shoulder, distracting her from her observations. "I have to pick up my boys from school."

Buddy and Noah took the opportunity to return to their table.

George smiled at Mel. "Wow, is it three already? Thanks for all your help today."

"Will you be in tomorrow?" Mel's tone made it sound more like an accusation than a question, but George let it go.

"If Olivia wants my help, I'll be here." George waved as Mel hurried toward the back door.

"Is she always a grouch?" Grace asked once Mel was out of earshot.

"It's just her way." George stared at the back door. Mel had stepped up and been cooperative and helpful. "I think she's probably a nice person with an unfortunate manner."

"So, you're a barista now?" Grace pulled a twenty-dollar bill from her black and gold purse.

"Apparently. What can I get you?"

"I'll have a sugar-free caramel latte with skim milk." Grace gave George a mischievous grin.

She was deliberately asking for something she thought George wouldn't know how to make. It was a test. The joke was on her. George had been considering buying an espresso machine. A cheap model. She'd been watching videos in preparation for her purchase. George filled the small filter with coffee and tamped it down, then she set it to brew.

Once she was finished making the latte, she placed it in front of her sister. "You didn't think I knew how."

"No, I didn't, but you looked so natural doing it." Dark circles shadowed her eyes, which she'd tried to hide with makeup.

"Is everything okay?" George asked. "This is a long way to come for a drink, especially in the middle of your work week."

"I'm fine." Her sister squeezed her purse tight, her knuckles turning white.

"Talk to me," George urged.

She placed her bag on the counter and pressed her lips into a thin line, seeming to think about her answer. Finally, she said, "Could I stay with you if I had to? Liam wouldn't mind, would he?"

"Of course." George would never turn Grace away. They'd grown up in a hellish home and had always been able to count on each other. "You're my sister. He'd be fine with it. What's going on?"

"I'm not sure. I could be imagining things."

"What kind of things?

Grace shook her head, her blond hair shimmering in the artificial light of the café. "I don't want to talk about it." She took a sip of her coffee. "This is good."

"That's what a coffee addiction will do for you." Liam appeared next to Grace.

George's heart hitched, the way it always did when she saw him. It had been nearly six months, and her reaction to him hadn't faded. She'd let Grace evade her questions for now, but sooner or later, her sister would tell her what was troubling her.

Liam held out a set of keys. "I had that budget meeting with the mayor and councillors. John asked if you'd lock up."

His eyes connected with hers in that heavy-lidded way that always made her wish they were alone. Then he winked. It was a promise for later. "What time do you get off?"

The place had quietened down considerably since she'd arrived. "Can you wait for an hour? It's been a long day. I know Olivia normally closes at seven this time of year, but I'm done in. I'll give it another hour and then close up." She pointed to Buddy and Noah who had returned to their table by the window. "Do you see that guy with Buddy?"

Liam leaned in close. "Who is he?"

"He went to school with Carly. You should go and chat with them. Grace will keep me company while I clean up."

Liam raised his eyebrows. "Am I supposed to ask anything in particular?"

George frowned. "I don't know."

CHAPTER THIRTEEN

"Hi, Buddy." Liam sat down, not caring if the pair in front of him wanted to talk to him or not. Georgina's intuition had been spot-on this morning, and he trusted her. "Is this your quiet time between boat season and snowmobile season?"

Georgina's childhood friend worked as a boat mechanic in the summer and fixed snowmobiles in the winter.

Buddy shrugged. "The weather's turning. We're supposed to get our first big dump of snow in a couple of weeks."

Liam frowned. They'd had a small sprinkling of the white stuff, but he hadn't heard anything about a big snowfall.

Buddy must've seen his expression because he laughed and then said, "At least that's what the snowmobilers are telling themselves."

"Georgina tells me you knew Carly." Liam held out his hand to Buddy's friend. "Sorry, I don't know your name."

"Noah." The young man's handshake was firm but not bone crushing. "We went to school together."

Buddy shook his head. "Are the pair of you treading on RCMP toes?"

Liam tapped the table to make his point. "What happened to Carly was bad. We're just helping them with their inquiries and trying to get a picture of who she was so we can find her killer."

"And George promised her mom," Buddy countered.

Liam ignored him, not wanting to comment on an active investigation any more than he had to. He especially didn't want to talk about Georgina's connection to the case. He addressed Noah. "Back to Carly."

Noah pursed his lips, thinking, and then said, "She was nice. Everyone liked her. She would've made a good teacher."

"Have you seen her much lately?"

"I used to see her when she worked at the Rockin Horse. Of

course, that was her spring and summer gig. Once September hit, she went back to the city. I didn't see her at all in the winter." Noah didn't fidget or avoid the question.

In Liam's experience, a suspect who was uncomfortable would maybe take a sip of their drink or look away. One woman he'd talked to when he was undercover had taken all her belongings out of her purse and stacked them in front of her. Noah, on the other hand, showed no sign that he had anything to hide.

"Did she socialize when she was here?" Liam asked.

"She used to, but I didn't see much of her this past summer. Word was she had some boyfriend she was into."

The secret boyfriend again. "What do you know about him?"

"Nothing." Noah shook his head. "She wouldn't say who he was."

"Could you give me a list of the people she knew? She might have talked to one of them."

Noah leaned back in his seat. "Sure. I'll make a list tonight and drop it off at the station tomorrow. It's not right what happened to her."

If Carly had been seeing Nathan Wells, she probably wouldn't have told Noah. From the way the young man talked, they weren't close, and she wouldn't have blabbed about her affair with a married man. Magpie was a small town. People would frown on that sort of thing. Maybe instead of wondering what Carly was like, he should start asking about Nathan Wells. "Hey, Buddy, you can fix anything, right?"

"Sure. I'm a certified Red Seal mechanic." Buddy had merely stated a fact without any hint of boastfulness. He was known as the best, and most honest, mechanic in town.

"So why do you work on boats in the summer and snowmobiles in the winter? Why not work all year round for Nathan Wells?"

Buddy's eyes narrowed. "Do automotive repairs, you mean?"

Liam nodded.

Buddy drummed his fingers on the table, considering his answer. "Because Wells seems nice enough, but when you get to know him, he's a dick. He inherited the business but has no idea how to strip down an engine. Plus, he's always looking for someone to blame. I've heard that he screams at his staff in front of the customers. If he did that to me, I'd punch him."

"Then I'd have to arrest you," Liam stated.

Buddy's eyes widened. "Awesome." His tone had a sarcastic edge. "I'm lucky," he continued. "I don't have to worry about a few slow months. When my dad died, he made sure my mom was in a good place financially. I don't need to worry about her. Besides, Harry Bawa's a great guy. Last Holi, he and his wife brought in food to celebrate with us, then he closed the shop."

"Holi? What's that?" Liam asked.

"It's the Hindu celebration of spring. We threw colored powder at each other and water balloons. Then we ate Mrs. Bawa's delicious food. It was a lot of fun." Buddy smiled. "Why do you ask?"

"I've always wondered why the best mechanic in town doesn't work on cars. But Bawa sounds like a great guy to work for." There was no way Liam would admit that Wells was on his radar. But if what Buddy said was true, why would a pretty, young woman with a bright future hook up with a jerk like Nathan Wells?

CHAPTER FOURTEEN

"I think Grace is unhappy with Rob. She asked if she could stay with us if she needed to. I said yes. You don't mind, do you?" George said as she sat at the kitchen table.

"Of course not. She should dump him. He's an asshole." Liam's head and torso were swallowed up by the freezer as he searched for something to cook for dinner.

She was exhausted after her long day. If it were up to her, she'd make do with a cheese sandwich, but Liam seemed to need more than that.

"Aha!" He held up a box of chicken fingers. "The RCMP are not sure Wells is the man in the photo with Carly." He grabbed a baking tray out of a drawer. "All we have is a man in profile. They've been trying to blow up the image, but the quality is too poor." He tore open the box and emptied the contents onto the tray. "We can't positively identify him."

"In other words, I shouldn't go to his garage and start asking questions." Which is exactly what she wanted to do. Nathan Wells should at least be interviewed, if only to eliminate him.

He set the dial to the desired temperature and placed their dinner in the oven. "If you do that, I'll have to arrest you." He turned to face her with his hands on his hips.

She waved away his obvious frustration. "Don't worry, I have to be back at the Jumping Bean at six in the morning, and God knows how long I'll be there. Although, I have to admit the idea of you cuffing me is a turn on." She grinned at him.

He straightened, giving her a wide-eyed stare. "Let's go." He crossed the room in two strides, grabbed her hand, and tugged her toward the bedroom.

She stopped in the hallway, faced the wall, and then placed her hands on the hard surface above her head. "You need to pat me down."

She heard him unzip his pants and then a low rustle, which suggested he was shrugging out of his clothes. He stood close behind her, so close she could feel his erection rubbing her backside through her jeans.

"Have you been bad?" He pressed small nips and kisses down her neck.

She bent her head sideways, giving him better access. "Yes."

He started the pat-down at her left ankle, working his way slowly up her leg. Her vagina contracted as his long fingers trailed her inner thigh. She gritted her teeth as he worked his way down her right leg without touching her intimately. Once he was done, he stood behind her. "I need to do a thorough search."

He drew down her zip and shoved her jeans down around her ankles, tugging her underwear with them.

She felt wonderfully exposed standing in the dim hallway, wearing nothing except a sweater and bra.

He trailed his fingers along her clitoris. As her nerve endings reacted to his touch, she arched back so her head was against his shoulder. He was like a live wire that lit her up. His touch, his scent, or a look. That was all it took for her to be ready and willing.

His free hand reached under her sweater and pushed her bra aside. He circled her areola and then thumbed her nipple. He goaded her with a slow and steady rhythm.

She didn't need any teasing. He could bend her over and enter her here in the hallway, and she would come. She groaned. "Oh, God, I love you."

He stopped cold.

Only then did she realize what she'd said. *Shit.*

He flipped her around to face him. "Did you mean that?"

She stared at the ground, not wanting to see the panicked look in his eyes. "Yes, but please don't freak out. You don't have to feel pressured. You don't have to say it back. It's not..." She wanted to say it wasn't a trap but couldn't. She had changed everything, and no matter what happened, there was no going back. She couldn't unsay those words.

Using his index finger, he brushed a stray hair from her cheek. "That's the first time you've told me you love me."

Tears gathered at the corners of her eyes, the depth of her feelings making them water. "I should have been honest with you." That was only partially true. She should've been honest with herself first.

"I love you, too." His mouth slanted over hers, his tongue exploring, plunging deeper.

She didn't have time to react to his words, and maybe she didn't need to. She felt his warmth, desire, and tenderness in the way he held her.

Everything had changed. They were no longer playing. This wasn't just sex; this was a joining, a commitment.

He broke the kiss and, without a word, he tugged her sweater up and over her head. She lifted her arms to help him get it off. Then she unhooked her bra and let it fall to the ground.

He held her hand and led her to their bed. She lay down, feeling vulnerable, not because she was physically naked but because she'd laid bare her love.

He stared at her and smiled. "You're all I've ever wanted." Then he stretched out on top of her.

She opened her legs to accommodate him. He reached between them and settled his erect penis against her opening. She expected him to thrust into her, but he didn't. He rocked in place, each movement penetrating a little deeper, but not deep enough. "Say it again."

"I love you. I love you. I love you."

He pulled out and then started over, tormenting her. Going a little deeper each time he entered her, but never enough.

She wanted more. Her breath coming in short gasps, as her need for him climbed.

He stopped, captured her arms and, using one hand, he held them above her head. He sucked her left nipple into his mouth and then started rocking again. Her body swirled out of control.

"More." She growled out the word. Her patience for play was

at an end, and every fiber of her being screamed for completion.

He released her hands and thrust into her, groaning as he buried himself to the hilt.

She wrapped her legs around his waist, her ankles digging into his lower back. Her hands had a death grip on his shoulders. She moved with him. He plunged into her, hard and fast. Her whole body was pulsating around his penis. With a shuddering scream, her control shattered into a blinding pleasure.

He let out a roar and pounded into her, giving way to his own orgasm.

"I love you, too," he panted into her ear as he collapsed on top of her.

She lay there, enjoying the heaviness of his weight pressing down on her.

He shifted onto his back. "If I don't move, I'm going to squash you." He tucked her against his side so she lay nestled against his muscled body, her head fitting into the crook of his neck.

"Did I hurt you?" he panted.

"No." Her body reacted to him in such a visceral way that she didn't think he could hurt her during sex. "Did you enjoy it?"

"It was great. You know what this means?" His voice had a throaty, hoarse quality.

"What?"

"You're stuck with me now."

She grinned. "Good."

He didn't say anything else, but she could tell he was smiling by the way his body relaxed. She released a long, cleansing breath, closed her eyes, and drifted off.

"Shit!" He jerked to a sitting position.

She tumbled to the side, grabbing the nightstand so she didn't fall out of bed.

He dashed naked out of the room. The oven door banged open. Only then did she realize they'd forgotten about their dinner in the oven.

She climbed out of bed, shrugged into her robe, and padded to the kitchen.

He gave her a lopsided grin that deepened the dimple on the left side of his face. "They're extremely well done, but I think they're edible." He tipped the chicken fingers onto a plate and placed it in the center of the kitchen table for them to share. He didn't seem to care that he was still naked, and she wasn't going to complain. It was always a pleasure to watch his toned body move with the lithe grace of an athlete.

She grabbed some plates from the cupboard and some plum sauce from the fridge.

"We need to talk," he said between bites. They weren't too hot for him.

"What's wrong?" She sat and broke a piece in half, waiting for it to cool so she could eat it.

He swallowed and then said, "We have to move closer to town."

"I know."

"Renting a place isn't forever. We can get a month-to-month lease. That way we can move whenever we want."

Suddenly, she wasn't hungry. "You're right. But the places we've seen are... I hated the apartment, and that last place was...yuck. I'm not a clean freak by any means." She waved her arms wide to encompass their home. "But when a house has a moldy kitchen floor, it's not livable."

"The mold can be cleaned." He took another bite. The conversation wasn't affecting his appetite at all.

"If there's that much dirt we can see, then how much is hidden? I'd rather live in the apartment than get sick in a place that has mold." She pushed her plate away, giving up on eating.

"We need a solution. Even if you do get your license back, we need to plan for the worst. What do you suggest we do?"

She placed her elbows on the table and rubbed her temples. "I don't know, but you're right. I was frozen riding into town yesterday."

"You know what I think...?" He hesitated, staring out of the window to the dark lake.

"Just tell me."

"I think you're scared to move because all this change is coming at you at once. You have epilepsy, you've lost your job, you can't drive...even I'm an adjustment. Although I like to think I'm a good one." He waggled his eyebrows.

She smiled and placed her hand over his. "You are."

"You're holding on to this place because it's the one thing that has stayed the same."

She leaned back in her chair. "Maybe you're right."

"Maybe?" He raised an eyebrow.

He was way too smug for her liking. "I'm not living in a moldy house, and you shouldn't want to either, which means your analysis is flawed."

"You have a point." He stood and gathered up her plate.

She got the sense he was placating her because he didn't want a fight, not because he believed she was right. "I'll do a search for houses tomorrow and see if there's any new listings, but we're limited to the town of Magpie, and there's not much available."

He placed the dishes in the sink and turned to face her.

She stood and returned the plum sauce to the fridge and then pointed to the dishes. "I'll wash them in the morning before I leave for the coffee shop."

"Was I wrong about the changes in your life?" Liam moved to stand behind her, wrapping his arms around her waist, poking her with his now erect penis.

"Yes and no." She grinned. "You failed to mention the biggest change."

He kissed her neck. "What's that?"

"All the sex." She placed her hand in his and led him to their bedroom.

CHAPTER FIFTEEN

Liam was tired, achy, and absolutely satisfied. The only thing that would make his life better was if he could spend the day lying in bed with Georgina. Normally, on a Saturday morning, he'd do just that. Unfortunately, she had promised Olivia that she'd open the Jumping Bean. He decided he might as well work and had headed for the Magpie Police Station after dropping her off.

He sat at his desk, working his way through a stack of tickets. He'd learned that by scanning through the infractions, he could identify repeat offenders and problems and hiccups in the system. There were some people in Magpie who went out of their way to make life difficult for their fellow citizens. There were others who just needed a little help.

One of his new officers, a constable by the name of Cote, had issued four tickets to seniors who hadn't shovelled their sidewalks after the last snowfall. While it was true that town bylaws stated pathways had to be cleared within twenty-four hours of the last flurry, Cote's tickets were excessive. As far as Liam was concern, Cote's actions were petty and just plain wrong. He would have a chat with the constable and set him straight. Maybe Liam could organize some volunteers to help out the elderly homeowners.

The phone on his desk buzzed. Jillian, who worked the switchboard on the weekend, said, "There's a Nathan Wells calling for you. Do you want me to take a message?"

"No, put him through." Liam grabbed a pad of paper and a pen as the line clicked. "Chief Mason here."

"Hi. This is Nathan Wells. I'd like to set up an informal interview." He sounded smooth and confident.

"What's it about?" Liam scribbled down his observations.

"Carly Hale."

Liam blew out a long breath. Nathan was bold. "Where are you now?"

"I'm at my garage. Do you know where that is?"

"On Main Street?" Liam's instinct was to never trust a person who offered up information without being asked. "I'll be there within the hour." He hung up and threw his pen on the desk. Then he picked up his smartphone and dialed Mia.

She answered on the second ring. "This is my day off. I'm spending time with my kids." Which translated to *this better be good or heads will roll.*

"I'm just keeping you in the loop." Liam kept his tone upbeat.

"About what?" she snapped.

"Nathan Wells called. He wants to talk about Carly Hale."

"That's interesting." The anger disappeared from her voice.

"Georgina thinks he's the man in the photo."

"Your girlfriend is perceptive."

He ignored her comment and continued, "I'd like to bring Georgina along. Her insight has been invaluable."

There was a long pause. He thought Mia might deny his request. Finally, she said, "I'll allow it because, technically, she's still a police officer, but you lead. She is there to observe only. And I want a full report once you're done."

"Got it." He disconnected and then called Georgina. "How's it going at the coffee shop?"

"The morning rush is over. I'm just clearing up." She sounded happy.

"How's Olivia?"

"Grumpy. She has a walking cast, but it still hurts. I've managed to get her to sit down with her foot on a chair to stop the swelling." There was a low hum of conversation in the background.

"Do you think she'll be able to spare you for a few minutes?" Liam asked.

"Hold on."

He heard a faint mumbling, which suggested that instead of muting the phone, Georgina had simply covered the speaker.

After a minute, she was back on the line. "No problem. Olivia says she'll be glad to get rid of me."

Liam suppressed a laugh. "Is she cranky?"

"So cranky," Georgina announced in a loud voice, which was obviously directed at Olivia who was, no doubt, listening in.

"I'll be there in fifteen minutes. We have an interview to conduct." Liam hung up before she could ask any questions.

****

George stared up at the familiar white brick building with black signage that declared *Wells Automotive*. She'd never set foot inside. Buddy had always worked on her car, and she'd never had a reason to come here in her capacity as a police officer.

Liam parked the Magpie Police Service SUV in front. "Georgina." Liam covered her hand with his. "I know you'll have questions, but save them. Mia's team will also need to interview Nathan Wells. Mia okayed your presence because you're still a cop, but you're here to observe only. You can take notes. Got it?"

"Got it." She would have loved to walk into the garage and force Wells to tell her what he knew, but that wasn't how investigations were conducted. She needed to hold her emotions in check if she was going to keep her promise to Susan Hale.

"I want you here because your observations are important." He let go of her hand and opened the SUV door.

George rummaged through the glove box until she found a pad and pencil, then joined Liam on the sidewalk.

Nathan Wells must have been waiting because he strode out to greet them, smiling. He shook Liam's hand and clapped him on the shoulder. There was a good-old-boy feel to Nathan's actions. He obviously thought of Liam as a peer, but didn't use the same tactic on her. He simply nodded his head in her direction and then ignored her, a slight she'd expected. In Nathan's world, she was nothing, a nobody, and he treated her as such.

Liam glanced at her, pressing his lips into a thin line, letting her know that he'd noticed the snub, but he wasn't going to say anything about it. She understood. He wanted Nathan to be forthcoming, and that was more likely to happen if they maintained a friendly attitude toward him.

She followed the two men into the building, jotting down her observations. Nathan was clean-shaven with short brown hair swept to the side. He wore a clean pair of black jeans and a black form-fitting jacket over his slim frame. His hands weren't those of a mechanic. There wasn't a speck of grease under his fingernails, and his skin was smooth with no callouses. It was unlikely he actually worked on the cars in his shop. Everything in his posture, from his straight back to the way he held his head high, suggested he was confident and had no reservations about this meeting.

The garage was a good size with six car bays, all of them full. It smelt of oil and engine exhaust. Nathan led them to his small windowless office at the rear of the building.

He sat behind his desk and pointed to two chairs on the other side. There were no files and no papers to indicate he did any work. "I'll get to the point. I know who killed Carly."

"How do you know?" Liam pulled out a seat for George next to the wall and then took the spot on the outside.

"Two weeks ago, she sent me a text, telling me it was over between us." Nathan placed his elbows on the desk and clasped his hands together. He seemed poised and affable, not upset at all about Carly's death.

"What was over?" Liam could've gleaned what Nathan meant from the context of the conversation, but he probably wanted Nathan to spell it out.

"Sorry, didn't I say? Carly and I were having an affair. I'm not proud of it, but it happens." He shrugged. "I showered her with gifts. Anything she wanted, I gave her, but that wasn't enough. She wanted me to leave my wife. When I refused, she dumped me." Nathan's answer felt rehearsed.

George jotted down his words along with her observations.

"Do you still have the text, or did you delete it?" Liam tilted his head.

Liam's demeanour was almost friendly and not as confrontational as she expected. It wasn't the way George would've played it given Nathan's admission. But she trusted Liam's experience and judgement.

Nathan fished his phone from his jacket pocket. He tapped the screen and then turned the device toward Liam, who scrolled down, reading the messages. George couldn't see them from her position, but Liam's frown told her that he didn't like this development. Using his smartphone, he took pictures of the texts.

Nathan tapped the desk with his index finger. "As you can see, she dumped me and ran off with this Tom person."

Liam leaned back in his chair and narrowed his eyes. "Tom who?"

Nathan shrugged again. "I don't know. All I know is what it says here."

Liam took a notebook out of his inside jacket pocket and flicked through the pages. As far as George could tell, they were blank. "This is a different number than the one her mom gave us. Didn't that make you suspicious?"

"The one ending in three fives?" Nathan cleared his throat, a sign that he wasn't as confident with this line of questioning. "I gave her that phone. She was mad at me so I figured she probably wanted nothing to do with me and bought herself a new one."

"Why was she mad at you?" Liam asked.

George guessed Liam was being deliberately obtuse and, in doing so, was forcing Nathan to talk about his affair with Carly.

"Because I refused to leave my wife," Nathan repeated. "I gotta be honest. It was a tough decision. I loved Carly, but with Elizabeth..." He drummed his fingers on the desk. "We have a history. I'm not ready to give that up. You need to find this Tom guy." Nathan poked the air with his index finger.

Despite Nathan's declaration of love, George still didn't see any sign that he was distressed over her death or the fact that her young life had been cut short by violence—a circumstance that would sadden anyone, but especially someone who had been intimately involved with her. Nathan seemed more intent on clearing his name. She added that observation to her notes.

"Don't worry. We'll look for him," Liam promised as he slid Nathan's smartphone across the table. "Does your wife know about your affair?"

Nathan blanched, his reaction too visceral to be faked. "No, and I'd be grateful if you didn't tell her."

"I can't make any promises. Unfortunately, with a suspicious death, these kinds of things tend to crop up in the course of an investigation." Liam stood and headed for the door.

George followed but glanced back to see Nathan watching them, assessing them. She had the distinct impression that Nathan Wells had laid out a path he wanted them to follow.

"So, what do you think?" Liam asked as he put the car in drive.

"He's lying," George stated bluntly. "Carly wouldn't have needed to go out and buy a new phone because she already had the one we found in her room. Can I see the text that she supposedly sent?"

"Sure." He pulled up in front of the Jumping Bean, tugged his phone out of his pocket, and scrolled to the images.

I've met someone else. Tom is a great guy. We're leaving together. Don't look for me—Carly.

"He did it." After reading the message, she had no doubt. It wasn't that she could say definitively that Carly didn't write it, but there was no personality to it, no details, no warmth. The young woman George knew had been warm, kind, and wonderful.

"Prove it. He's just given us reasonable doubt. The only physical evidence we have in the case are some generic sandbags and rope. The sandbags are sold at every gas station and hardware store. The same can be said for the rope. Carly was in the water too long for forensics to get any fingerprints. Because of this development"—using his thumb, he pointed behind him—"we now have to chase up every man named Tom that Carly knew or might have known."

"So we can refute his claim?"

"Yes. I'll see if the RCMP can track down the new phone. It's probably a burner, but it still needs a service provider. Once we know which company that is, it won't be too hard to find out where it was purchased. If we can find out where it was obtained, we'll have a piece of the puzzle."

CHAPTER SIXTEEN

Saturday afternoon shift at the Jumping Bean was quiet. There were no tourists at this time of year and only a few locals stopped by on the weekend. The lack of business worked in George's favor because she was still processing this morning's interview with Nathan Wells.

She had finally persuaded Olivia to go home and take a nap. *Thank God.* Olivia's sunken eyes and pinched expression revealed just how much pain she was suffering. Normally, she was an energetic, cheerful soul who could be a little too blunt, but her physical state had made her an ill-tempered grouch.

In between customers, George called everyone she could think of who'd known Carly. She started with Buddy's friend Noah. He answered her questions and then texted her a list with the names and numbers of their mutual acquaintances, the same list he'd apparently sent to Liam. Those friends gave her names and numbers of a few more people. Within a short while, she'd reached out to nearly fifty of Carly's acquaintances.

No one had ever heard of Carly hanging out with a guy named Tom. Unfortunately, none of them had heard of her having any romantic relationships at all. George knew Carly had a love life because Nathan had admitted to being her lover. How had she kept it a secret? In a small town, no less.

Everyone George spoke to said the same thing: Carly didn't socialize. Some of the people George had contacted had suspected there was a secret man. Others didn't care. Carly had just stopped hanging out with her high school friends, and they had never asked why.

It was nearly closing time. She scrubbed down the counters and started to clean the espresso machine. If only they had a witness who'd seen something... She stopped what she was doing. They did have someone who had observed a woman who had shown up at Carly's dorm and threatened her.

George did an internet search to find Nathan's wife. Elizabeth Wells was a real estate developer and one of the people behind the push to deregulate and develop the public lands east of town, the same place where Carly's body had been found. Could that be only a coincidence?

George downloaded Elizabeth's profile picture and then dialed Liam. "Can I send Jackie Jones a photo of Elizabeth Wells?"

"You have her photo?" He sounded surprised.

"Social media," she said, giving him the short answer. He would've probably gotten there himself, but he'd been dealing with all his usual work while helping her keep her promise to Susan Hale.

"It'll be better coming from me." There was no censure in his tone, just the bald truth. He was the police chief of Magpie. He had authority.

"Okay. Call me back when you hear from her." She hung up.

He called within ten minutes. "I sent Jackie a collection of images, all blondes. She identified Elizabeth Wells. You know what this means?"

She nodded, but then realized he couldn't see her, and said, "Nathan's wife knew about his affair with Carly. Which makes me wonder if Elizabeth Wells kept her knowledge a secret from her husband. Or did Nathan lie to cover for her?"

CHAPTER SEVENTEEN

As Liam drove twenty minutes east of town to Nathan and Elizabeth Wells' acreage home, he was distracted by thoughts of a house that had come on the market in Magpie, but it was for sale, not rent. It was at the point on Lakeshore Drive where the paved road ended. The lot was dotted with mature trees and overlooked the lake. It would be perfect for them. But he wasn't sure how Georgina felt about that kind of commitment.

"What time do you have to be at the Jumping Bean?" Liam broke the silence with a neutral question.

"I was vague. I said I would be there in the afternoon and stay until closing. It's Sunday, so I'm not expecting it to be busy. Did you run a check on Nathan and Elizabeth?" Georgina stared out at the fields. There had been a dusting of snow, but the higher clumps of dirt could still be seen above the sprinkling of white.

"Yes. They've been married for eight years. They have no kids. The wife, Elizabeth, is a self-made woman who's a real estate developer. There are firearms registered to Nathan, two hunting rifles, two shotguns, and five handguns. From the records, I gather all the weapons are antiques apart from the rifles."

She raised an eyebrow. "He's a collector who also hunts, and she has money."

"He's not exactly poor either. He inherited his money from his dad. Although, I think it's safe to say she's the brains," Liam added.

The wrought iron gate that guarded the estate was open, so they drove up the long, winding driveway. There was a pond on their left with a non-functioning ornamental fountain. Liam suspected the sprays of water had been turned off for the winter. Three cars were parked in front of the house. The Wells' either owned a lot of cars or they had visitors.

Elizabeth opened the front door as they parked in front of

the three-car garage. She wore expensive jeans matched with an equally pricey skin-tight sweater. Her clothes probably cost more than Liam earned in a week. Jackie Jones had been spot-on with her description. Elizabeth Wells looked expensive.

Two men and a woman emerged from the residence. Bruce Koval and Anna Wiebe were realtors who were on the town council. They were also investors in the wetlands development.

Liam considered their professional careers and their work in public service to be a conflict of interest. How could they act in the best interests of the community, and at the same time use their position to push through proposals that allowed them to build on public land? But as far as he knew, they hadn't done anything illegal.

Liam and Georgina climbed out of the SUV and walked towards the house.

Koval ignored them as he marched past, heading to his SUV. He was a sour man who rarely smiled and complained about everything. He had a generous waistline with gray hair and matching moustache. Liam estimated he was in his late fifties.

The last man through the door was James Stilton, the manager of the golf course. He'd been present at the crime scene when they'd recovered Carly's body. His attendance here could just be a fluke, but his presence did put him on Liam's radar.

Stilton adjusted his glasses, ran a hand over his smooth bald head. He nodded in Liam's direction and then headed for his truck.

Anna Wiebe reached her vehicle and greeted them with a bright, vivacious smile. "We're planning our Christmas dinner at the golf course. Will you be attending?"

She wore her white hair short and spiky. Her bright red winter jacket and black pants looked as classy and professional as always. Liam guessed that she, too, was in her fifties.

Liam faked a smile. "Sounds good. Email me the details."

He couldn't imagine anything worse than spending time with these people.

"Why are you here?" Elizabeth Wells snapped at Liam from

the doorway.

"We'd like to talk to you about Carly Hale," Liam answered in a sharp tone. If she thought she could intimidate him with her bad temper, she was wrong.

"Oh, thank God." She smiled; her relief palpable. "Nathan's out hunting, and I thought he'd had an accident." She waved them inside.

Georgina stepped back and let Liam go first, once again assuming her role as observer.

Elizabeth led them through a light, airy foyer into an equally bright sitting room that had pale gray walls, white molding, and maple hardwood floors.

Liam pointed to a tall black safe that sat in the corner of the room. "Is that your gun safe?"

"Yes, it is. Do you want to check our arms and see if they've been fired?" Elizabeth rolled her eyes to emphasize her sarcastic comment.

"Sure, if you're offering." He didn't need to check the firearms in the house, but he never turned down an offer to inspect someone's weapons. He couldn't seize them. No one had been shot, and they had no bearing on any investigation to his knowledge. But it was good to know who had what when it came to guns.

Elizabeth huffed and then crouched over the keypad so he couldn't see. She punched a few buttons, and the safe door clicked open.

"I like your earrings," Georgina said as Liam checked the weapons. He wasn't sure if she was distracting Elizabeth or if she was genuinely interested.

"Thank you." Elizabeth's voice had softened.

"They're different, like a ruby is dangling in a silver cage." Georgina leaned closer to get a better look.

"It's a garnet in a platinum cage," Elizabeth corrected.

"Platinum, wow! I don't know anyone who owns platinum jewelry."

Elizabeth pulled at her earlobe and then flicked the dangly

earring. "My husband bought them."

As far as Liam knew, Georgina wasn't into bling. He placed the firearms back into the safe. Once they were done here, he would ask. That was the kind of thing a boyfriend should know. He decided to bring the conversation, and his thinking, back to the subject at hand. "Is your husband aware that you know about his affair with Carly Hale?"

"I have no idea what he knows or doesn't know, but I think he suspects that I know." Elizabeth dismissed the idea with a wave of her perfectly manicured hand.

Liam blinked as he worked his way through her word maze. "You've never had an open conversation about it?"

"No." She shook her head. "Some things are better left unsaid."

"But you had no problem going to Carly Hale's dorm room and threatening her," Liam pressed.

"That's different," Elizabeth spat, allowing her anger to show. "I didn't get where I am by letting people take what's mine. Nathan gave that little gold-digging bitch everything. I'm the one who's married to him. That little slut was just after what she could get."

"Slut?" Georgina shouted. Her hands balled into fists.

"Georgina." He was shocked by her outburst even if he understood her outrage. But this was a police interview and a certain amount of professional restraint was expected.

She paced to the window, her back ramrod straight. She was too close to this case, too emotionally involved, and barely holding on. Perhaps bringing her here was a bad idea. They needed to take a step back before she lost her self-control.

"Thank you for your time. We'll let ourselves out." Liam grabbed Georgina's elbow and ushered her toward the door.

Once they were in the car and driving down the highway, she sighed and then said, "I'm sorry. I shouldn't have lost my temper. I blew it."

He couldn't help but smile. "Actually, you just raised your voice. You didn't verbally assault her or anything, which was good because we'd have been screwed."

"That's true." She stared out the passenger window, avoiding eye contact.

"To be honest, I'm just glad you didn't punch her," he said, trying to lighten the moment.

She snorted and gave him a small smile. "It was tempting."

He gripped the wheel tighter. He was as conflicted as she was. He wanted to make her feel better when he should be chewing her out for her behavior. "I appreciate how you feel, but you've got to control yourself. We would have got more out of her if—"

"If you hadn't been forced to shove me out the door." She turned to face him, biting her lip, a sign that she wasn't feeling good about her actions.

"Right." He softened his tone. "You need to look at this from Elizabeth Wells' perspective. Carly was sleeping with her husband."

"Yes, but she wasn't a slut. The girl I knew, the woman she became, wasn't a gold digger. She was just nice…a good person. It's hard to listen to someone talk about her like that. Especially since she's dead."

"So should I get you earrings for your birthday?" He forced a smile, changing the subject.

She frowned. "I don't have pierced ears."

"You're not into jewelry?"

She laughed and then said, "You're surprised I asked about Elizabeth's earrings?"

"Yes, are they important?"

"I don't know. They're familiar. I think I've seen them somewhere. Maybe Grace has a pair. I don't know. They're platinum and garnet. Is garnet a valuable gemstone?"

He shrugged. There were a multitude of gemstones of varying values. "I know about the main ones, diamonds, sapphires, rubies and emeralds, but I have no idea about the rest. And I'd never be able to tell if one was a fake."

She put a finger to her lip. "I'll have to do some research."

CHAPTER EIGHTEEN

Olivia sat at her spot near the rear of the café with her injured foot up on a chair. The place was empty when George arrived. There wasn't even a dirty dish on a table, which suggested there hadn't been any patrons for quite some time.

George slipped off her coat, hung it on a rack in the back office, and then joined her friend at the table. "There's no one here. Why are you in today?"

"Because I put out a notice telling my customers I would be open on Sundays until the end of October. Normally, I use this time to put up my Halloween decorations." She pointed to her ankle. "But that's not happening."

"I could help." But the idea of sticking up skulls, or whatever, to Olivia's exacting standards, filled her with dread.

"God no." Olivia slapped the table, implying George's suggestion was the most outrageous thing she'd heard all day.

"That was blunt." She loved her friend dearly, but Olivia was being a little too honest.

Olivia patted George's hand. "You are a wonderful, intelligent, caring, talented woman, but you have no eye for design. The fact that you look gorgeous is a fluke of nature."

George blushed. "You think I'm pretty?"

Olivia gave her a look that suggested she'd lost her mind. "Everyone does."

"You know you're still hot." She was uncomfortable with this turn in the conversation.

Olivia gave a self-satisfied smile. "Like most women, I work at it."

George couldn't argue with that because she had no idea what that would entail. "What do you know about Bruce Koval, Anna Wiebe, and James Stilton?" she asked, wanting to talk about something more important.

Olivia crossed her arms over her chest. "Why should I know anything about them?"

"Because your husband is the mayor?"

"John told me some things in confidence," Olivia said, stalling.

"Someone killed Carly Hale. Maybe they killed her to protect a secret."

She pursed her lips together and then said, "This is my observation, you understand, but Bruce used to be a lovely man. Lately, he's the meanest jerk you'd ever want to meet. I don't know why he changed."

That might be something, but then again, it might not. It was hardly worth killing over. "And Anna Wiebe?"

Olivia inhaled sharply and then said, "She seems nice."

"But?" George knew there was more.

"John says she always gets her way on everything. If she wants something to happen, she makes it happen." Olivia clapped a hand over her mouth, seemingly shocked by her own words.

"How?"

Olivia's shoulders slumped.

"I promise you this won't come back on John. I just want to understand who these people are and if they have any connection to Carly's death." George gave Olivia's hand a squeeze.

Olivia sighed. "There doesn't seem to be any one way, rhyme, or reason to her method. Some councillors will side with her on one issue and then different councillors will team up with her on the next one."

"But she always wins."

"Always. John's been looking for a common denominator, but he can't find one."

"And Elizabeth Wells?"

"I haven't heard much about her except she's behind the development of the wetlands." She pounded her fist on the table, her anger obvious.

"You don't approve?" George couldn't contain her surprise.

"Why do we have to fill in the wetlands to build condos?" Olivia was almost shouting.

"I'd have thought you being a businesswoman, you would've wanted to develop the area."

"People don't just come here for the beach. They come to watch the birds, too. By destroying the wetlands, we're reducing the number of visitors who'll come to the area. Why can't they be built somewhere else? I thought public lands were owned by all Albertans and not just something that could be sold off."

"Public land, or crown land, is owned by the province. In fact, sixty percent of Alberta is crown land. Most are recreational areas, like the wetlands, but they are not designated as parks and, as such, are not protected in the same way."

"It seems to me there are a couple of town councillors who are getting rich off land that's supposed to belong to all Albertans."

George didn't comment. She had no idea that Olivia was so passionate about the new condos. They had never discussed it. The truth was, George hadn't really thought of it at all. Local politics wasn't her thing. "Is there anything else you can tell me?"

Olivia released a long breath, seemingly in an attempt to calm herself. "You can't mention this to a soul, not even Liam. John hasn't been able to prove anything, but he suspects government officials were bribed by Elizabeth Wells to get the approvals for the wetlands development. But questioning something is different than knowing. He has no proof. He also thinks the town books have been doctored." She leaned in close. "He's asked the Alberta Ombudsman to look into it."

George stared at Olivia, trying to sort through the information. "Are you saying that John suspects Elizabeth Wells is corrupt? And that he has no idea how Anna Wiebe always gets her way? Plus, Bruce Koval used to be nice but is now a mean jerk."

"Yes, that's what I'm saying."

George drummed her fingers on the table. Did any of this add up to a motive for murder?

CHAPTER NINETEEN

George walked to the police station after she closed the Jumping Bean. The sun was setting behind her, casting long shadows on the sidewalk. The wind had died down, making it a cold but pleasant evening.

This should be an enjoyable stroll through a picturesque town, but she was troubled by her actions at Elizabeth Wells' house. In retrospect, they hadn't been that bad. She'd just been a bit too sharp with Elizabeth, but it was a sign that she was emotionally compromised. If she was going to help Susan Hale find closure, she needed to get her act together.

Liam had decided to catch up on some paperwork. At least, that was what he'd said in his text. But she knew he was working on a Sunday so they could ride home together. *Damn.* It was mid-October, and the daytime high was minus ten, which wasn't that cold. She was safe from frostbite because she had the right clothing and good boots. It would be a different story come January and February when the temperature could dip to minus forty. Once Olivia was back on her feet and the police had figured out what happened to Carly, George would put all her energy into getting them a place in town. Hopefully, they could move by the beginning of December.

"Well, look who's here for a visit." Jake smiled from behind the glassed-in reception desk as she entered the building.

"Hi. How are you keeping?" A pang of longing hit her hard in the chest. She wasn't part of the team and didn't belong here anymore.

"I hear you've been helping Olivia out at the Jumping Bean." Jake seemed genuinely interested.

"It's keeping me out of trouble," she admitted.

"Liar. You're looking into that nasty business with the Hale girl."

"You know about that?"

"The whole town knows." Jake was a strict officer who had always been somber and serious. He seemed happier now than he had in the past. Maybe his mood had more to do with Liam's leadership than her presence.

George grimaced. She was uncomfortable with the idea that her involvement with the investigation was common knowledge. But then again, Mia, the RCMP, and Liam knew what she was doing and hadn't objected. That was good enough for her. She pointed to Liam's office on the other side of the glass. "Is he in?"

"Yep. I'll buzz you through." He pressed a button under his desk, which released the electronic lock.

She walked down a short hallway to find Liam's door ajar, but she knocked anyway.

His face lit up when he saw her. "Come in and shut the door. I have something to show you." He pointed to a smartphone on his desk.

She closed the door and made herself comfortable in one of the visitors' chairs. "What is it?"

"Mia had a clone of Carly's phone delivered. She said it wouldn't hurt to have another pair of eyes on it."

"Have they found anything that links Carly to Nathan or Elizabeth Wells?"

"Nothing. I think that's why Mia sent it to us. She's desperate. I can understand that. By the way, I forgot to tell you the medical examiner's report came in. Carly was struck in the head, probably with a hammer. There was no alcohol in her system and her stomach was empty."

George squeezed her eyes shut for a moment, trying to block the images the report conveyed. She took a deep breath and focused on the cloned device. "We know she was having an affair with Nathan Wells."

Liam scanned the report. "But there's no physical evidence linking him to the crime. We also know Elizabeth Wells threatened her, which adds another suspect to the list. But once again there's nothing to prove Elizabeth did it."

"Has Mia had any luck tracking down this mysterious Tom?" George reached over and plucked up the clone. She scrolled through Carly's list of contacts.

"The man she purportedly ran off with?" he clarified and then shook his head. "No. They're tracing the number, trying to match it to a purchase. Once they do that, they might be able to find out where it was sold, and from there, hopefully, discover the buyer."

"Look at this." She turned the phone toward Liam. "She knew a Tomás. He's in her phone contacts. We should check him out."

"Seriously?" He shook his head. "That took you all of five seconds. Mia's team is slipping."

CHAPTER TWENTY

They rose early to drive the two hours into Edmonton. Liam needed to be back for work. George hadn't made any definite commitments to Olivia, but she would drop in and see how things were going once they were done in the city and were back in Magpie.

Two trips in one week. This was the most she'd traveled outside of Magpie since June. Even though it was winter, she loved the commute. The dusting of snow on the fields, the trees along the highway, and the sight of the river valley as they crossed the North Saskatchewan River, all made her feel like a tourist who was here to explore the city. And not someone who was here to discover who had killed her friend.

This time, they parked in one of the public parking lots near the University of Alberta Administration Building. Liam wore his uniform, which helped smooth the way with the staff. They were given Tomás Sheehan's schedule and tracked him down in the Medical Sciences Building as he was leaving his class.

Liam identified himself and then said, "We'd like to talk to you about Carly Hale."

"Me?" Tomás seemed surprised to see them. "I hardly knew her." His long dark hair was tied in a dishevelled ponytail. He wore a scruffy black T-shirt with the name of a band emblazoned on the front and a skin-tight pair of blue jeans.

Liam made no comment. He simply stared at Tomás, waiting for a reply.

"Can we grab a coffee while we talk? I overslept and haven't had my caffeine dose for the day," Tomás said, filling the silence.

"Sure." Liam glanced in her direction, arching an eyebrow.

She supressed a smile. He knew she would never turn down a cup of java.

"How did you know Carly?" Liam asked as they joined a long

line for the coffee shop in the lobby.

"We did a few projects together." Tomás' gaze scanned the room, not making eye contact with Liam.

"You never saw her outside of school?" Liam scrutinized the young man.

Tomás shrugged.

Liam gritted his teeth, took a deep breath, and then said, "That's not an answer. Someone took Carly's life." Using his index finger, Liam poked Tomás in the chest. "Do I need to question everyone you know in order to get a response? Because that won't go well for you. No matter what, people will wonder if you had something to do with her death. And that kind of mud sticks."

Tomás blanched and then held his hands up in surrender. "I'll admit, I used to have a crush on her. She was sweet and cute. We did a few art projects together, and I asked her out."

"What did she say?" Liam's voice had an edge to it. He was out of patience.

Tomás sighed. "She said I wasn't her type."

"And you left it at that?"

"Of course, I'm not a creep." Tomás seemed offended by Liam's question.

"I want to see your phone," Liam demanded, holding out his right hand, waiting for compliance.

Tomás fished his device from the back pocket of his jeans.

Liam pressed the home button and then turned the screen to face Tomás. "Unlock it."

The young man did as he was asked. Surprisingly, he wasn't as nervous now. Maybe having a crush on Carly was his big secret, and once it was out in the open, he had nothing to fear.

"Using his own phone, Liam took a few pictures and then passed it back.

"For the record, I'm dating Jackie Jones," Tomás stated.

"The same woman who lives across the hall from Carly?" George said, wanting to make sure she understood what he was saying. Jackie had mentioned that Carly had done a few projects with her boyfriend.

"Yes." Tomás nodded. "We've been going out for six months."

"Six months? When did you ask Carly out?" Liam heaved a sigh, allowing his frustration to show.

Tomás tilted his head to one side, thinking, and then said, "Eleven months, two weeks, and three days ago. Look man, I'm sorry about what happened to her, but it had nothing to do with me."

****

Liam didn't talk until they turned onto the highway. "He has an alibi for the date and time that the text was sent to Nathan Wells. There are messages were he's setting up a hockey game with his friends. He would've been playing when that text was sent.

"So why did you take pictures of his phone?" George smacked her dry lips together. They hadn't waited in the long line for coffee. Liam had ushered her out as soon as the interview was over. She couldn't blame him. It would've been awkward if they kept standing there once they were done.

"The photos I took prove where he was and who his friends are, should we need to ask. Plus, the message wasn't sent from his number. We don't have an exact time of death, but we do have a time stamp for that goodbye text that was sent to Nathan. I believe it was sent after she was killed."

"Tomás could have another cell phone. He might have taken a break in the game and sent it then."

Liam signaled and turned off the highway at the edge of the city limits. "That's possible, I suppose, but I don't think he's our guy. In fact, I don't think Tom is real."

"Neither do I. I guess it's another dead end. Unless Mia's team can track down the phone that sent that text." She swivelled her head, trying to get her bearings. "Where are we going?"

He grinned. "To find a coffee shop. Do you really think I'd drive all the way home without getting you your fix?"

She smiled back at him. "You really are an awesome boyfriend."

CHAPTER TWENTY-ONE

George hummed as she savoured the slightly bitter taste of her latte. She had thought of Carly as a studious, quiet person who wanted to be a teacher. Never once, had she imagined Carly as the kind of woman who would date a married man.

She placed her drink in the center console cup holder. "Can I see Carly's cloned phone?"

He fished it out of his inside jacket pocket and passed it to her. "Are you looking for anything in particular?"

"Not really. I just find it hard to believe there isn't something on here that can help us. Oh, and while I'm thinking about it, someone needs to question Nathan about Carly's third phone. Well, I guess it would be the second one she owned."

His eyes slanted to her momentarily and then switched back to the road. "What?"

"If Nathan is to be believed, Carly had three phones; the one she used for everyday business, the one that sent the goodbye text—"

"And the third one?" He frowned.

"As far as I can tell, she never sent texts or called Nathan... ever."

He rolled his eyes and slapped the stirring wheel. "Of course. That's so obvious. She must've had a phone just for Nathan. He probably had a dedicated device, too. because the only message she ever sent to his regular device was the goodbye one."

"Exactly. There are three phones in the mix. We've accounted for the first one." She held up the cloned phone. "The RCMP are trying to track the burner that sent the goodbye text, but there's no evidence of any communication between Nathan and Carly, and yet he has admitted to having an affair with her."

He cocked his head to one side, his eyes still on the road. "In which case, why did she send the goodbye text to his regular phone?"

"She didn't because she was already dead," George stated. "It keeps coming back to Nathan Wells." She rubbed her tongue along the roof of her mouth, trying to rid herself of the bad taste that had suddenly materialised.

"I'll call Mia and get her to check Nathan's service provider and see if she knows how they communicated. Maybe they didn't text, but they might have called each other." Liam steered the police SUV onto the shoulder and snagged his phone from his jacket pocket.

While he was talking to his former boss, George scrolled through Carly's photos. There were pictures of her mom, Jackie, Cindy, her classmates, and loads of selfies. She stared at the smiling face of the young woman whose life had been snuffed out too soon. In one picture, taken last Christmas according to the time stamp, she wore a black sheath dress that accentuated her curves. Her hair was up, revealing drop silver earrings.

George gasped. "I knew I'd seen them before."

Liam disconnected his call. "Seen what?"

She enlarged the image. "Those earrings. They're a red gem in a silver cage."

"They're the same ones Elizabeth Wells was wearing?" he asked, his voice rising.

"Yes." George couldn't contain her excitement. They had a lead.

Liam's brow creased. "Elizabeth Wells said they were garnet."

"You think the gem is important?" she said, trying to figure out what he was thinking.

He narrowed his gaze as he stared off into the distance. "I don't understand why anyone would put a garnet in a platinum earring."

"A cheap stone in an expensive setting." She shook her head. "That seems more like bad taste than a crime."

"No, it's a personalized taste," Liam stated.

"And if it was personalized, there had to be a reason. I'm googling garnets now." She pressed her screen. "Top hit—it's the

January birthstone. There's a wide range of them. I'm not sure what that means. Blah, blah, blah...they tend to have a brown tint, which makes them less valuable than other red gems like rubies."

"January birthstone... How much do you want to bet that Carly's birthday was in January? I'll get Mia to look in the files." He pulled out his phone again and sent a text.

George patted his arm. "Get her to find out Elizabeth's birthday, too."

Within a few minutes, his phone gave a high-pitched, hollow ringing sound, telling them Mia had replied.

He read the text. "Carly's birthday is New Year's Day, and Elizabeth was born in April."

George googled a list of birthstones. "April's birthstone is a diamond. Why would a materialistic woman like Elizabeth Wells wear a garnet instead of a diamond?"

"If I had to guess, I'd say it was a powerplay. She's sending Nathan a message." He signaled, checked over his shoulder, and then steered the vehicle back onto the highway.

"What would that be?"

"I killed your girlfriend."

CHAPTER TWENTY-TWO

"What do you want?" Elizabeth Wells snapped as she opened the door to her impressive home.

They'd driven to the Wells estate before stopping in Magpie. George had promised to hold her temper, no matter what Elizabeth said about Carly. She just hoped she could keep that promise since Elizabeth seemed to be able to provoke a response. Maybe it was her sense of entitlement and the idea that people like Carly and, by extension, George, were somehow less worthy. But she had to consider the possibility that Elizabeth was inciting a reaction in order to distract them. If that was the case, they were dealing with a very cunning woman.

"Can we come in?" Liam asked. "We need to talk to you about the death of Carly Hale."

Elizabeth curled her lip into a sneer. "I'm on my way out. You'll have to come back later."

"You don't understand. You can talk to us here or at the station." Liam stepped inside, refusing to take no for an answer.

"Don't you need a reason?" She crossed her arms.

"You're in possession of a dead woman's earrings." Liam's eyes narrowed. "That gives us a reason."

"Oh, that." She led them through the house to the same sitting room they'd visited earlier.

She flopped down into an over-stuffed cream-colored leather armchair.

"Can you tell me how you came to be in possession of Carly's earrings?" Liam didn't sit.

George followed his lead and positioned herself by the window.

"I found them in Nathan's truck."

George briefly made eye contact with Liam. Most people would balk at wearing a dead woman's jewelry, especially one who'd been murdered. Elizabeth Wells was not most people.

"Did you know they belonged to Carly?" Liam made his voice stern and forceful.

"Of course, I knew." Elizabeth looked like she wanted to laugh. "She was leading him around by the nose, and he couldn't see it. Why shouldn't I have them? He gave that bitch everything, money, clothes, a phone, and his time. He was so damn besotted. I took her stupid earrings. A girl like that doesn't deserve them."

"You went to her dorm and threatened her. Did you kill her?" Liam whispered. His cold gaze was laser-focused on Elizabeth.

"No," Elizabeth roared, her eyes wild. "I didn't have to kill her. She was nothing, a nobody. A waitress and a cleaning woman at a hotel. She couldn't support him. I told him if he left me, I'd take everything. He would be broke." She poked the air with her finger to emphasize her point. "And if there's one thing Nathan can't handle, it's being poor. There was no way he was going to leave me for her. If you ask me, that little bitch got what she deserved."

"Are you saying she deserved to die?" Liam said through clenched teeth, a sign that his control was slipping.

"She made it happen. She should've known her place," Elizabeth screamed.

Liam balled his knuckles into a fist.

George closed the gap between them and grabbed Liam's elbow. "This interview is over. You will be hearing from the RCMP." She tugged at his arm, making him leave.

Once outside, she gulped down a big lungful of air, hoping that it would somehow cleanse her insides.

Without a word, Liam unlocked the car. She could see the muscles in his jaw twitching as he fought for control.

"I feel like I need a shower." George snapped the seatbelt in place.

"Me, too." Liam climbed into the SUV beside her. "I wish I could arrest her for being a nasty, evil, toxic woman."

"I wish you could, too," George admitted. Elizabeth was probably one of the vilest people she had ever met, and that included her drug-dealing psycho father. "But she did make a good point."

"What was that?" Liam started the car.

"She didn't have to kill Carly. She could just divorce Nathan. It's her money," George reasoned. "But she did tell us something useful."

"She confirmed that Nathan bought Carly a phone." He glanced at her and then switched his gaze back to the road. "Where do you think it is now?"

"My guess would be the bottom of the lake." George shook away the image of Carly's body, cold, wet and bloated. "Do you think Elizabeth could have done it?"

"I'm not ready to strike her off the list yet." Liam turned at the end of the driveway, heading to Magpie.

"Why not?"

"She's not just angry; she's enraged. She was jealous of Carly. She mentioned the time he spent with her." He tapped the steering wheel, making his point. "She's still a suspect. Where to now?"

"I promised Olivia I'd check in on her. Just drop me off. I'm sure there'll be something to do."

CHAPTER TWENTY-THREE

Liam was met by a frowning desk sergeant when he entered the Magpie Police Station. Jake Taylor tended to be gruff, but lately he'd been showing signs of mellowing. Some days, he was positively cheery. Today was not one of those days.

"What's wrong?" Liam approached the desk.

Jake growled as he nodded toward the seating to his right.

Liam turned to see Anna Wiebe and Bruce Koval. Wiebe, who was normally pleasant, had her hands clasped in her lap and glared at Liam. Koval's lip curled into a sneer.

Both stood and stomped toward him in unison.

"We need to talk to you," Koval snapped.

There was something about their attitude that made the hairs on the back of Liam's neck stand on end. He was about to be attacked. He didn't take his gaze off them. "Jake, is interview room one available?"

"Yes," Jake barked.

Wiebe, Koval, and Elizabeth Wells had plans to build condos on the land next to the golf course. What if they'd killed Carly because she'd discovered they'd were doing something illegal? Maybe Carly's death had nothing to do with an affair. Perhaps it was about good old-fashioned greed. "Can you please show Ms. Wiebe and Mr. Koval the way?"

Jake buzzed all three of them into the station.

While Jake took the pair of town councillors to the interview room, Liam went to his office, turned on his computer, and scanned the reported incidents from the last few days. Nothing jumped out as an issue worthy of a visit from a pair of town VIPs.

Jake knocked on the open office door. "They're ready when you are, and they've asked for coffee, preferably in to-go mugs."

Liam gave Jake a quizzical look. "Where do they think they

are?"

"Hunt used to cater to them. I'll go and get their drinks."

"No, you won't. We are here to protect and serve the people of Magpie, not the special interests of the town council. And I'll be damned if any of my officers will play at being their waitstaff." Liam stood and headed out of his office. "You will come with me. I won't tape the interview because they're not suspects, but I want you to take notes. The time for special favors is over."

Jake grinned. "I like the way you think."

Liam entered the gray scruffy interrogation room first. Wiebe and Koval sat at the table, which had a bar across the middle to accommodate restraints. Liam and Jake each took a seat opposite.

"Chief Hunt used to see us in his office," Koval spat.

Liam crossed his arms and said nothing. He just waited. This was a power play, and he wasn't going to buckle. They had to speak first. He refused to beg them for information or cater to them in any way.

"I'll get to the point." Anna Wiebe brushed imaginary crumbs off the table.

"I suggest you do." Liam managed not to bark, but it took all his control.

"We want you to stop harassing Nathan and Elizabeth Wells." Bruce Koval slammed his hand down on the table, acting like a tough guy. "They're good people, especially Elizabeth. She's donated a lot of money to the town." The look of uncertainty in Koval's gaze told Liam his actions were all bluster.

Liam leaned back in his chair and considered Koval's words. When he proclaimed Elizabeth had donated money to the town, what he probably meant was that she'd donated funds to get him elected. Liam suspected a businesswoman like Elizabeth Wells would own votes on the town council.

He leaned forward. "You do realize this is a homicide investigation?"

Anna Wiebe cleared her throat. "We understand that, but it's hardly a matter for the Magpie Police Service, is it?"

He turned his gaze on her and was gratified when she flinched. "We are working in coordination with the RCMP."

Koval sneered, "We made you police chief. We can take the job away."

Liam suppressed a laugh. "Are you saying you'll fire me if I don't drop a homicide investigation?"

"I wouldn't have put it like that, but yes. Carly Hale was a gold digger. A girl like her was lucky to get attention from a man like Nathan." Koval glared at Liam, not backing down.

A girl like her. Koval's words echoed Elizabeth's.

"'Lucky?'" Liam smacked the table, losing the last shreds of his patience. "She's dead. Someone dumped her body in the lake. That's not lucky."

"The Wells have standing in the community." Anna Wiebe held her head high, haughty now. "They matter."

"The implication being that Carly didn't," Liam whispered. No wonder Susan Hale had begged Georgina to look into Carly's death. These people controlled the narrative, and the story they were selling was one that depicted Carly as a throwaway person.

Anna Wiebe coughed and then said, "Well, I wouldn't exactly say—"

"Jake, get them out of my sight." Liam stood, pointing to the door. "I serve the people of Magpie, not you." Liam stormed out of the interview room, strode to his office, and slammed the door.

A few minutes later, there was a knock and Jake entered. "They're gone."

Liam pointed to the chair, telling him without words to sit. "You got all that in your notes, right?" He paced around the room, fighting to get his anger under control.

"Every word."

"Damn. If I'd known they were trying to obstruct an investigation and that my job would be threatened, I would've recorded it." He slumped down in his chair and stared at Jake. "Did you know that was going to happen?"

Jake gave a slight shake of his head. "What are you going to do about it?"

Liam rubbed his temples. "I'm going to call the RCMP, Alberta Justice, and the Solicitor General. I'll make a report so everything's on file. Then I'm going to resign."

CHAPTER TWENTY-FOUR

George ran steam through the milk steamer nozzle on the espresso machine, wiped down the counter, and then grabbed a gray dish tub and set to work bussing the dirty dishes. Olivia had posted a list of items that needed to be accomplished in the evening so the hectic mornings could go off without a hitch. It was now an hour before closing time, and George had decided to get a head start on her evening chores.

"This job suits you," Olivia called from her seat near the bathrooms. She'd been here all day with her foot propped up on a chair, watching over her kingdom.

George laughed. "I don't know about that, but I do like feeling productive. How's your ankle?"

Olivia made a yuck face, revealing her frustration. "The swelling has gone down, and it just aches now."

"As opposed to?" George grabbed two glasses that had once held frappés and a now empty coffee mug. She added them to the tub and then cleaned the table, making it ready for tomorrow's customers.

"A knifing pain."

George winced. "Ouch. So you just slipped on the ice?"

"Yep, all it took was a moment. I was lucky I didn't break my neck. It puts things into perspective."

"In what way?" George moved to the next table.

"I understand why John keeps nagging me to retire."

"You've never mentioned this." She hated the idea of Olivia not being a part of her life.

"Because I was ignoring it. When you're young, you feel invincible. As you age, you get twinges and aches that you ignore because you want to keep on going. But, in reality, it's your body telling you to slow down."

George stopped what she was doing, left the bus tub on a

table, and joined her friend. "What will you do?"

"I haven't decided. John wants us to spend the winters somewhere warmer."

"Like the States?" Many Canadian seniors wintered in the US.

"That's one option, but I like the idea of southern British Columbia."

George's mouth suddenly felt dry. A dull ache started in the pit of her stomach. What could she say? If Liam had stayed in the RCMP and been transferred to another province, she would've gone with him. She couldn't stand in the way of her friend's happiness. "Will you sell the Jumping Bean?"

"I suppose I'll have to." Olivia's gaze wandered about the café.

"Makes sense. The money will come in handy." George swallowed, trying to bury her emotions for her friend's sake, if nothing else. "I'll miss you." They were simple words that didn't begin to describe the hole Olivia's absence would leave in her life.

The electronic door chime sounded, letting her know a customer had entered. She leaned to the right to see Nathan Wells and James Stilton, the manager of the golf course. *This should be interesting.*

She rose and walked to the till. "What can I get you?"

"I'll just have a large coffee," Stilton replied, his manner indifferent.

"Do you want room for cream?" George made sure her tone was crisp and polite.

"No, black is fine."

She poured the coffee into a mug, passed it to Stilton, and then addressed Nathan Wells. "And for you?"

"I'll have a large vanilla latte."

She rang in the order and then set to work making Nathan's drink.

"I thought you were a cop," Nathan said, loud enough so the whole café could hear, not that there were any other customers.

"I am." George maintained her tone, not allowing him to get to her.

"Do your bosses know you're moonlighting? Isn't that against some sort of rule? What would they say if they knew?"

This sounded like a veiled threat, and there was no way she would put up with that. "Moonlighting would suggest I'm earning money. I'm not."

"We're expected to believe you're just doing this out of the kindness of your heart?" Nathan sneered.

"I'm helping a friend who's injured."

From the corner of her eye, she saw Olivia lever herself to her feet and hobble in their direction.

Stilton had taken his coffee and was heading for the door. George added vanilla syrup to a to-go mug and then poured in the espresso and steamed milk. She handed it to Nathan, hoping he would take the hint and leave.

"I'm going to lodge a complaint," Nathan grumbled.

"You do that." Olivia waved a fist at him. "I'll be happy to allow the powers-that-be to go through my books and prove that I haven't paid George a penny. Since when is it a crime to help out a friend?"

Nathan snatched up his drink and followed Stilton out.

"What was that about?" Olivia asked once the door closed behind the two men.

"It was about friends helping friends." George stared after them, wondering just how close Nathan Wells and James Stilton were.

CHAPTER TWENTY-FIVE

Liam nearly tore the door from its hinges as he entered the coffee shop. He wanted to relax for Georgina's sake but couldn't. The more he thought about the meeting with Koval and Wiebe, the harder it was to contain his anger.

He made a beeline for Georgina who was sitting with Olivia at the back of the café.

"Olivia, I need you to cover. Georgina and I need to talk in private. Can we use the office? Thanks." He didn't wait for a reply. He was too wound up, too agitated, to care.

"What happened?" she asked, the moment the door was closed behind him.

He paced to the filing cabinets that sat against the far wall. The space was small with just a desk in the middle of the room. "Remember those two councillors that were at Elizabeth Wells' place?"

She frowned. "The ones who are in real estate? What about them?"

"They threatened to have me fired if I keep questioning Nathan and Elizabeth Wells." He balled his hands into fists at the memory.

Her gray eyes widened. "They want you to compromise the investigation?"

"Yes."

"Why would they do that unless the Wells' are guilty? Those jerks are trying to cover it up." She stood with her hands on her hips.

"I thought the same. I've reported it to the appropriate authorities. Wiebe and Koval will probably be charged."

"That's awesome." She sat on the desk. A slow smile curled her lips as her anger dissipated.

He closed the distance between them and wrapped his arms

around her so her head was level with his chest.

He kissed her head and then said, "But we still have no physical evidence linking Nathan or Elizabeth to Carly's death. We don't even know where she was killed." Just holding her made him feel calm and in control.

She widened her legs to accommodate him and tugged him closer. They comforted each other for a few minutes, then she stared up at him. "We should check out the golf course."

"Why? There's no reason to think Carly was killed there."

She pursed her lips and then said, "This might be nothing, but Nathan was in with James Stilton, the manager of the golf course."

He frowned. "And that's suspicious because…?"

"Because when Olivia broke her ankle, she called me for help."

He gave her a look that hopefully suggested she'd gone crazy. "I'm not following."

She sighed, probably wishing he was smarter. "It's human nature for us to rely on our friends or, in this case, cronies. Who would you go to if you were in trouble?"

"You," he answered without hesitation. "What's your answer to that question?

"You." She gave the same rapid-fire response. "But if you were hurt, I'd call Grace, Buddy, Olivia, Greg, or Alan."

"That's a decent list." He smiled.

Her eyes shone in the dim room. "It's a lot longer than it was a year ago."

He forced himself to concentrate and not get distracted by her changeable eyes, her scent, or the intimate way she was holding him. "And you think when Nathan was in trouble, he got a friend to help him out."

"Maybe." She furrowed her brow. "But we can't assume Stilton was automatically a party to murder. Do you know what's been bothering me?"

"No." He sniffed her hair, enjoying the scent of coconut. "But you're going to tell me."

"I can't picture Nathan and Carly's relationship. They were

lovers."

"That's been established." Once again, he had no idea where she was going with this.

"Where's their nest?" She leaned back, snagging his gaze.

"Their what?"

"They're love nest. I can't see them doing it in the back of a car every time. Once or twice maybe, but all the time?"

"Her dorm room? That's where Elizabeth made a scene." He hadn't thought about Nathan and Carly's relationship in that much depth. He'd been looking for evidence and tracking mysterious non-existent boyfriends.

"That worked when Carly was in school, but what about when she was working here for the summer? Her mom said she stayed out all night and would never say where she went."

"A hotel," he said, stating the obvious.

"Maybe, but it would have to be out of town, and it would have left a paper trail. I'm not sure Nathan would've wanted that."

She made a good point.

"Or Nathan could ask a friend for a favor. Ah, yes..." It had taken him way too long to understand Georgina's thought process, but she was right. Nathan and Carly must have had a place to go. "I like the way you think."

She placed her hands on his chest, forcing him to take a step back out of her embrace. "We should take a look around the golf course."

"We'll check it out, and if we find anything, we'll call Mia, but first I have to quit my job." She didn't flinch at his words or show any sign that she was upset, but he needed to know that she understood the ramifications of his actions. "Are you okay with that?"

She stood. "One of the reasons I love you is because I know you'll do the right thing. If the corrupt councillors expect you to bend to their whims, you'll never be happy here. You have to leave. You have no choice."

"And you?" He held his breath, scared of her answer.

She cupped his cheek. "I'd very much like to stay with you."

He rested his forehead against hers. "That means a lot to me."

She held his hand and tugged him toward the door. "We have to leave. Olivia needs her office to lock up for the night." She snagged her smartphone from her pocket and glimpsed at the screen. "It's too late to talk to John this evening. The town hall will be closed. Let's go home. You can talk to John in the morning. Then we can go to the golf course and check it out."

CHAPTER TWENTY-SIX

"If we go to a city that has transit, I won't need to worry about having a license." George placed their Chinese takeaway on the stove.

Liam grabbed a beer from the fridge. "How are you okay with this?"

She took two plates from the cupboard and placed them on the table. "To be honest, I'm not, but I don't want to stay here without you." She collapsed onto a chair.

Liam crouched down in front of her, concern in his dark eyes. He wrapped his fingers around her cold hands. "We'll make this decision together. I thought I'd try and find work in Edmonton. That way you can be close to Grace."

"I like that idea." The weight that had been centered on her chest lifted a little.

A knock sounded at the door.

Liam rose to get it.

"My bat is by the door." She smiled, knowing he would never use it.

"I don't need a bat," he said over his shoulder. "I'm not a wuss."

That made her laugh.

Moments later, Mia entered the kitchen. Liam followed closely behind.

"You don't seem upset that Liam has to quit," Mia barked. She was famous for her temper, but it had never been aimed at George.

George stood, readying for a fight. "For the record, I'm angry. We were just discussing our options."

Liam stood between them. "Okay, calm down both of you. Remember what this is all about. Someone is trying to cover up Carly Hale's murder."

"Sorry," Mia mumbled and then addressed Liam. "I just hate to see you in this situation." She fell into a seat.

"Would you like some food? There's lots here." George fetched another dish and then placed the takeout containers on the table. She poured everyone a glass of water to go with their meal. Finally, she joined them. She'd let Mia's outburst go. Liam's old boss must've jumped in her car and driven to Magpie as soon as he'd called. George suspected that Mia saw Liam as her protégé and was very protective of him, even though he no longer worked with the RCMP.

Mia grabbed a pair of chopsticks and emptied some steamed rice and chicken chop suey onto her plate. "Thanks. I'm starving."

Liam filled Mia in on their planned trip to the golf course while he helped himself to the sweet and sour spareribs. "Have you had any luck tracing the phone that sent the breakup text to Nathan?"

Mia swallowed her mouthful. "Not yet. You should know I'm taking Wiebe and Koval in for questioning tomorrow. My people are getting things organized as we speak."

"That's fast." Despite her quick-draw temper, George had to admit she liked Mia.

"We're also looking into their purchase of public land." Mia had an aura about her that suggested not only that she couldn't fail, but she had no idea what failure meant.

"I bet it's dodgy," Liam added.

A rhythmic knock sounded at the door, and a small distant voice called, "It's John King."

"And Olivia," her friend added. "He was supposed to tell you I was here, too."

George grinned.

Liam stared at George and then at Mia. "This'll be interesting." He rose to let them in.

John King, the mayor of Magpie, burst into the house the second Liam opened the door. "Don't quit. I refuse to accept your resignation."

"You know then?" Liam waved an arm, beckoning them into the living room.

Olivia limped in after her husband. Her face was pale, and there was a sheen on her brow.

"Olivia, for God's sake, sit down." George rushed to her side and helped her to the overstuffed armchair near the window. "What are you doing here?"

"I didn't want to miss any of the action." Olivia gave George a tight smile.

John eyed his wife, held up his hands, but then let them drop to his sides, an action that revealed his frustration at the futility of trying to get Olivia to do anything she didn't want to.

"You were saying?" Liam pressed, bringing the conversation back on track.

"Four police officers have already been in and another four have called. They're threatening to strike."

"Really?" Liam took a step back, his eyes wide. He glanced at George and then a slow smile spread across his face. The men and women of the Magpie Police Service wanted him to be the chief and had taken action to see that he remained in the job.

"Yes, sir. I've assured them that Koval and Wiebe will go before you do." The words rushed out of John's mouth.

Mia joined them in the living room. "In that case, I need you to call Alberta Justice and register a complaint. They'll investigate. We'll let them decide if laws have been broken. I already know they tried to interfere with an investigation. They will be brought in for questioning shortly."

"I'll call first thing in the morning, and I'll update the Alberta Ombudsman. I already have a complaint on file with them." John pulled a tissue from his pocket and mopped his brow.

If Liam was surprised by John's admission, he didn't show it. George felt bad that she hadn't told him, but it had been Olivia's secret about the councillors and wasn't hers to tell.

Liam inhaled and folded his arms across his chest. "Does this mean you support my investigation into Carly Hale's homicide?"

"Of course." John gave his head a slow shake. "That poor girl."

"Okay." Liam rocked back on his heels. "Tomorrow we're back on the job."

John moved toward the door.

"Is that it?" Olivia grumbled as she levered herself out of her seat. "I thought there'd be more excitement."

"Wait." George held up a hand, stopping John in his tracks. "Am I right in thinking that the town of Magpie owns and runs the Magpie Golf Course?"

He nodded. "That's right."

"Do we have permission to search the buildings and grounds for any sign that Carly Hale was there or was killed there?" Mia demanded. She had obviously followed George's train of thought.

"Yes," John agreed.

"Will you put that in writing?" Liam asked and then winked at George.

"I'll email you something as soon as I get home." John stood back, allowing Olivia to go first.

"Olivia," George called. "I'll be at the Jumping Bean as soon as I'm finished at the golf course. Rest your leg."

"I will, dear." Olivia eased down the steps toward their car, which was parked behind Mia's.

"I should go, too." Mia shrugged into her coat and stepped onto the deck. "I promised my husband I'd be home tonight. If I drive really fast and put the sirens on, I should get there in time to tuck the kids into bed." She marched to her SUV. "Call me if you find anything,"

Liam waved goodbye as he closed the door. "That was an interesting evening."

CHAPTER TWENTY-SEVEN

The Magpie Golf Course, which was a fifteen-minute drive west of town, was a massive property. Liam had checked a map before driving out here. The lot was basically a rectangular shape with the south side backing onto the lake. A clubhouse, restaurant, pro shop, and maintenance garage all sat at the north end of the property.

He parked near the maintenance shed. The corrugated metal building was massive enough that it could probably hold three buses and have room to spare. The place seemed deserted. Not a surprise given the freezing temperatures and the light snow cover. The town opened up the golf course to cross country skiers in the winter, but there wasn't enough of the white stuff for that yet.

"Let's check the shed." He shoved the letter from the mayor authorizing their search into his inside breast pocket.

They climbed out of the SUV. Liam led the way across the gravel parking lot toward the maintenance shed.

Georgina tugged at the handle on the industrial-sized sliding doors. They didn't budge. "Locked." A fine mist wafted into the air as she spoke. She looked good in her jeans and her heavy dark blue coat.

"Aren't all daughters of criminals supposed to be good at picking locks?" he teased as he stood on tiptoe, peeking through the side window.

She snorted and then said, "Dear old dad was more about intimidation than finesse." She closed the gap between them. "Let's see if there's another entrance."

They made their way through an alley that separated the shed from the clubhouse until they finally came to a rear door. Liam tried the handle and was pleased when it creaked open. "Hello." He stepped into the darkened interior. "This is the police," he called, not wanting anyone to think they were up to no good.

Two rows of golf carts were lined along the left side of the shed, and three mowers were parked near the sliding doors. A small storage room was located on the right-hand side of the building.

Georgina peeked inside. "They have sandbags." She entered the room and waved at a stack of ten on her left.

He followed her. "And they have yellow rope." He pointed to a coil that was almost hidden behind an industrial vacuum.

"Do you think they'll match?" She examined the rows of shelving that lined the back walls. There were assorted tools and hardware scattered about the cluttered space.

"Hard to say. We'll let the crime scene techs figure it out."

She'd finished walking around the room and had circled back to stand with him. "It's not proof, is it? Everyone who owns a truck has sandbags to add weight to the rear wheels in winter."

"Agreed."

"What are we looking for?"

"I hoped to find something that would help with the investigation. Maybe a red or reddish-black stain on a wall or a floor." He raised one eyebrow. "Failing that, a card that reads *Carly Hale was here*. That would be nice."

"Good luck with that." Georgina left the storage room, heading back into the main area of the garage.

Liam followed, but stopped when he saw the wooden handle of a tool lying on the ground behind the door. The place was such a mess that he wasn't surprised to find a tool out of place, but something inside him knew. It was the same gut instinct that had kept him alive when he'd worked undercover, and he'd learned to listen to it. He pushed the door closed to get a better look.

A hammer with a black stain on one end lay on the dusty cement floor. There seemed to be some hair stuck to the blunt end. He didn't pick it up. He inched the door open, being careful not to hit the hammer and called, "Have a look at this."

She edged back into the room and glanced down at the implement. Her face paled before she stepped back into the main part of the maintenance shed so it was out of her line of sight. "If that's the murder weapon, then leaving it on the floor behind a door was just stupid."

"It must've fallen here, and they didn't notice or else they would've dumped it in the lake with the body. The autopsy report said that Carly was struck once on the jaw and then twice on the head."

Georgina flinched, going even whiter, which he hadn't thought was possible. "Carly was probably facing her attacker. Otherwise, why hit her in the face at all? Why not just come at her from behind, smack her on the back of the head, and be done with it? I think we can assume she was struck in the face first." She put a hand to her stomach and swallowed hard.

Liam forced himself to picture the scene in his mind. "Okay, say you're right. She was hit in the face. She falls down. The two smashes to the back of her head are to finish her off. She might not have bled with the first blow, but two hits to the head would have bled a lot."

Liam pulled his phone out from his inside jacket pocket. "Hi Mia, I'm at the golf course. I think we have the murder weapon. Can you get a team down here to look for blood splatter?"

****

George calmed herself by making dragon breath in the cold air as they waited outside the rear door of the garage for the RCMP forensic team. She tried not to think about the hammer, or Carly, or death.

"You know there's a house near the community center that's for sale. It's a bit rundown." Liam blew into his hands to warm them.

"The last one on Lakeshore Drive before you hit town?" She pictured the house. It was bigger than their current home, and it was in a great location. "It caught my eye, too, but I dismissed it because it's for sale. I don't have enough saved for a deposit."

"It's close enough to town that you could walk, but it's on a large treed lot. It would be perfect for us. And I think we've been living together long enough that we need to have a talk about money."

"My side of that conversation will be awful short." She had no savings. In fact, she'd just finished paying off her student loans.

He scratched his jaw. "I probably should have told you before. I have a good amount saved."

"Money from your family?" The last time she'd met his parents they had been rude to her. There was no way she wanted to take their money.

"No." He shook his head, smiling. "I worked undercover for years. That's years of collecting a salary and not having much in the way of personal expenses. I saved a lot."

The sound of footsteps crunching on the ice and gravel alerted them that someone was walking along the alley. They hadn't heard any cars approach so there was no way it was the RCMP.

Liam inched to the edge of the building and peered around the corner. "It's James Stilton." He rushed to the club manager, not giving him time to get away. "Do you know who I am?"

George followed but said nothing.

Stilton nodded. "I've seen you around. You're the chief of police for Magpie. What are you doing here?"

"We're waiting for the RCMP to investigate a potential crime scene."

Stilton tried to dodge around Liam. "I have work to do, and you're not going to stop me."

Liam grabbed his upper arm. From the way Stilton winced, George assumed it was a biting grip.

"Are you obstructing a police investigation? Because I can arrest you for that," Liam barked.

Stilton paled. "No, but you don't have the authority to search the place."

Liam let go of Stilton's arm, reached into his inner pocket, and pulled out the mayor's letter. "Your boss, the mayor, has given me permission to search these buildings and grounds for any evidence linking this place to Carly Hale's death." He stepped closer, caging Stilton so he was trapped against the wall of the shed.

Stilton sneered, "He can't do that."

It struck George as bravado.

Liam tilted his head, paused for a minute as he assessed Stilton, and then said, "Judging by your hostility, you have something to hide. If that's the case, I will find out what it is and charge you. Then your lawyer can argue the point of whether this letter is valid in court."

"Wait now, I never said..." Stilton tried to back away, but he had nowhere to go. "I'll cooperate."

"When did you last see Carly Hale?" George asked.

"On a Sunday about two, maybe three, weeks ago." His lips trembled.

"Was she with anyone?" Liam's voice was harsh and forceful.

Stilton flinched. "Yes, she was with Nathan."

"Nathan who?" Liam stepped forward, crowding Stilton's personal space.

"N-Nathan Wells," Stilton stammered. His fear was obvious.

"How did they seem?" George kept her voice calm, a contrast to Liam's.

Stilton held his trembling hands up in a position of surrender. "I just saw them from a distance. I didn't talk to them. There's a room in the attic above the clubhouse. We keep it for... you know...for special guests."

She gasped. "That must be their love nest."

Liam ignored her outburst and focused on Stilton. "Who do you mean when you say 'special guests'?"

"Certain VIPs in town who want to have some fun without their spouses finding out. They pay me to keep the place clean and look the other way."

Liam poked Stilton in the shoulder. "Who are these VIPs who use the attic?"

"Nathan, Elizabeth, Anna, and Bruce." The words tumbled

out of Stilton's mouth.

"Just the four of them? No one else?" Liam confirmed.

"They bring people here. I don't know who their friends are." He ran a shaky hand over his bald head.

The sound of tires crunching on gravel rang through the air.

"Mia's here," George said, stating the obvious.

"Good." Liam stepped back so he was no longer crowding Stilton. "Now we'll be able to check out the attic."

CHAPTER TWENTY-EIGHT

Stilton unlocked the doors to the clubhouse. The restaurant was located on the left and the pro shop sat straight ahead. A spiral staircase was positioned in the center of the room next to a reception desk. The interior was tastefully decorated with dark hardwood floors, expensive molding, and pale gray walls.

Liam's gut told him that this was the place where Carly had been killed. He just prayed for Georgina's sake that someone had cleaned up the blood.

"As you can see, everything's closed for the winter." Stilton nodded toward the dining area and then led the way up the curved steps. He didn't make eye contact, which made Liam suspect Stilton knew more than he was letting on.

Once on the second floor, they followed the manager through a banquet hall to a door at the far end. Stilton needed two keys to unlock the bolt. The door opened to an unpainted wooden staircase. They climbed the steps to the third-floor apartment.

The moment they opened the door, the stench of bleach burned Liam's nostrils. He took two steps into the room to stand beside Stilton. The space was as tastefully decorated as the main floor with the same dark hardwood floors and cabinets and pale walls. The main room held a couch, a coffee table, and a granite counter with a hotplate and a kettle. To the right was a bedroom that contained a king-size bed and a connecting bathroom.

Georgina stayed at the entrance and scanned the area, not touching anything. "They scrubbed it down."

"Did you clean up the evidence with bleach?" Liam wanted to slam his fist into Stilton's face. "You must've known something was going on. You should've come forward. A girl is dead."

"Are you going to arrest me?" Despite the chill in the room, beads of sweat dribbled down Stilton's forehead.

Liam stepped back. He didn't want to assault the idiot and endanger the case. "The RCMP will hold you for questioning. They will then present the evidence to the crown prosecutor, who will decide if charges are laid."

"You said that just Nathan and Elizabeth Wells, Anna Wiebe, and Bruce Koval use this place?" Georgina addressed Stilton. Her voice was flat, suggesting she'd buried her emotions.

"Yes, Nathan, Elizabeth, Anna, and Bruce," Stilton confirmed.

"You mentioned that Nathan brought Carly here. What did the others use this place for?" She was laser focused on Stilton, which was probably a protective measure on her part. Concentrating on the case prevented her from thinking about how Carly had died.

"How should I know?" Stilton wailed. He sounded like a whining toddler.

"You know because they were all paying you off. Why else would you help them cover up a murder?" Georgina snapped out the words.

Liam realized that she hadn't buried her feelings at all. She was simply controlling her rage.

Stilton stared at the ground, seeming to sulk.

"If you cooperate, I'll speak to the prosecutor," Liam said, giving him an incentive to talk.

Stilton rubbed his eyes and then stared straight ahead. He looked like he might cry. Finally, he said, "Bruce likes men."

"That's hardly a crime." Liam stated the obvious.

"He's married to a woman," Stilton explained. "His wife doesn't know about his extracurricular activities."

"And he wants to keep it a secret, which makes him susceptible to blackmail," Georgina clarified.

Stilton nodded as he hung his head.

"And Elizabeth?" Liam asked.

"She's had several meetings with top civil servants and a government minister. I don't know what they get up to." Stilton still wouldn't look either of them in the eye.

"What about Anna Wiebe?" Georgina asked.

"She comes here alone every Monday morning. It's my day off, and she thinks I don't know." He tapped the side of his nose, finally meeting Georgina's gaze. "But I do."

Liam grabbed Stilton by the collar and was gratified to see real fear in the older man's eyes. "Did you kill Carly?"

"N-n-no. I just helped Nathan get rid of her body and clean up the blood."

"Tell me about the hammer." Liam tightened his grip, almost lifting Stilton off the ground.

"One of the cupboards was off its hinges. I was fixing it and left my tools here, but I didn't kill her, I swear." Snot ran down Stilton's face as he sobbed.

"How did it end up in the maintenance garage?" Liam fought to control his rage. Stilton had dumped Carly Hale's body in the lake.

"We must've dropped it when we were grabbing the stuff we needed." Stilton let out another sob.

Liam released his hold and inhaled sharply. They now had enough to arrest Nathan Wells.

"Liam, are you up there?" Mia shouted from the bottom of the stairs. Her voice had an edge to it, making her sound angry.

"Yes," he replied, matching her tone.

She stomped up the steps, grumbling to herself.

"This is where Carly Hale was killed," Liam said as she reached the apartment.

She stood beside Georgina and wrinkled her nose. "Bleach."

He nodded. "Exactly."

She waved them out of the room. "Okay, retrace your steps. I want you out of here. I'll get the techs to go over it."

CHAPTER TWENTY-NINE

George tucked her hand into Liam's elbow. She was huddled with Liam and Mia outside the clubhouse while the crime scene techs went through the third-floor apartment. Stilton sat in handcuffs in the back of an RCMP SUV. She hoped he served time in prison. He claimed not to have killed Carly, but he had dumped her in the lake like she was a sack of garbage. The caring young woman George knew deserved so much more than that.

George cleared her throat. It wasn't her place to sum up what they had, but she wanted to get it straight in her mind. "It appears that she was killed in the clubhouse. Then Stilton and Nathan carried her to the maintenance shed where they got the sandbags and rope."

"And they dropped the hammer," Liam added.

George nodded and continued, "They used one of the golf carts to take her body to the lake. Then weighed her down and placed her in the water." George couldn't bring herself to say Carly's name, which was crazy because it was obvious who they were talking about, but she needed the distance to function.

Liam pressed his lips into a grim line. "It looks that way. But which one of them did it, Nathan or Elizabeth?"

"Or both?" George said, speculating.

"The evidence points to Nathan," Mia announced. "Stilton's confession puts him at the scene of the crime. We also tracked the phone number that was used to send the *Tom* text. It belongs to a device purchased at a gas station in Edmonton. We have the date and time of the purchase, and we have Nathan Wells on surveillance video, buying the phone with cash."

"You're thinking he killed her in a crime of passion and then sent the texts to cover it up by claiming she'd left him." Liam stared into the distance. "Are you sure you have nothing on

Elizabeth?"

Mia shrugged. "She might have done it. Or she could've known after the fact. We'll have to interview them separately and see what we can get out of them. But we just don't have enough evidence to charge her."

A crime scene tech dressed head to toe in a white disposable paper-like suit exited the clubhouse, walked up to Mia, and whispered in her ear.

She nodded, acknowledging him. He then turned and went back the way he'd come.

"So far it seems that Georgina's hypothesis is correct. There are traces of blood and hair on the hammer and one of the golf carts. There's also blood splatter on the walls of the attic bedroom. There'll need to be a DNA analysis, which will take time, of course. And we've yet to identify all the fingerprints in the room."

"We should walk down to the shore and see if there's anything down there," Liam suggested.

Liam and Mia led the way with George following behind. The reality of what had happened to Carly was getting to her. How could someone smash Carly's head in with a hammer? It just made no sense. Nowadays, people got divorced, affairs ended. Killing someone in a moment of rage was one thing, but cold-bloodedly dumping their body in a lake was another.

The shoreline wasn't tended or manicured. It was a mass of reeds and mud. There was only one route to deeper water, and that was an old wooden dock, which was so ancient it might even predate the golf course. Rotten, warped planks held raised nails that stuck out like a trap, waiting to scratch someone and give them tetanus.

George held her breath as Liam inched out onto the rickety decking. He stopped about six feet out and inspected one edge. "I think that's blood. She must've gone in here."

"Okay, you can come back now," George ordered, not caring if she was out of line.

Mia pulled out her phone. "I'll get the techs down here, too.

And we'll bring Nathan and Elizabeth Wells in for questioning."

CHAPTER THIRTY

George got a ride to the Jumping Bean with an RCMP officer who was doing a coffee run. She'd left Liam and Mia to deal with the crime scene. It was police business, and she was no longer a cop. In fact, she'd never been that kind of a policewoman. George's stomach turned. She couldn't stop thinking about Carly's last moments. Had she died quickly? Had she known what was happening?

Olivia was busy, hobbling around on her walking cast, serving her customers. George helped herself to a coffee and sat at a table near the washrooms. She'd take over in a minute, but first she needed to rid herself of the bone-deep chill that froze her to the core. She didn't take off her coat, but sat cradling her mug with both hands, warming her fingers. It wasn't just standing outside for hours that had made her so cold; it was the reality of Carly's death.

Maybe she had enjoyed the excitement of having an affair with a married man, or perhaps she'd really been in love with Nathan. Either way, she didn't deserve to have her head bashed in and be dumped in the lake.

After a few sips, she started to thaw. A mother sat at one of the tables by the window, sharing hot chocolate and muffins with her kids. The boy and girl were loudly discussing their Halloween costumes. George closed her eyes and listened to their laughter, letting it wash over her. It was a reminder of all the good in the world.

She couldn't stop the bad things from happening, but she was now certain Carly Hale's killer would be brought to justice. Susan Hale would have her closure.

"Tough day." Olivia limped over to her table. Her face was pale and pinched, just as it had been last night.

"It could be worse." She tried to fake a smile. "You should sit down with your foot up." George stood and slipped off her coat as Elijah, the librarian, entered the café.

"I'm fine," Olivia snapped.

"Liar." George easily beat her to the till. "What can I get you?" She smiled at Elijah.

"A cappuccino." He grinned at her. "Olivia, are you staying off that ankle?"

"I wish everyone would stop fussing," Olivia grumbled, still working her way toward the counter.

"If you would take care of yourself, we wouldn't have to fuss," Elijah countered.

"I can ban you from my coffee shop," Olivia said. It was a half-hearted threat. Good-natured Elijah was a fixture.

"Ignore her." George set a small cup under the espresso machine. Then she addressed Olivia. "I've got this. Go sit down." George made sure her tone was stern but not bossy.

The act of brewing coffee grounded her, making her feel that she was part of the town, a living, breathing community, and not someone who knew the details of a friend's homicide.

The door banged open, and Nathan stomped in. His eyes were feverishly bright. His hair stuck out at odd angles, and he was unshaven, a different man than she had met a few days ago.

She heard a scream from one of the kids by the window. It was only then that she noticed Nathan had a handgun.

George ducked down behind the espresso machine, snagged her phone from her jeans pocket, and hit Liam's number. "Nathan's here. He has a gun." She poked her head up to get a better look.

Nathan aimed his weapon at her. "Hang up."

George placed her device on the counter, but she didn't disconnect the call. She just hoped Liam had the presence of mind not to talk.

"I heard you arrested Stilton." Nathan's voice sounded nasally, as if he'd been crying.

"How did you know?" George asked, inching her way to the end of the counter.

"It's a small town. Word gets around. Everyone knows." He waved the weapon at her. "Hands where I can see them."

She raised her arms in the air. "Tell me about Carly. You really loved her, didn't you?"

"Yes. I was going to leave Elizabeth for her." His voice cracked.

From the corner of her eye, George could see Elijah helping Olivia and the rest of the customers to the rear exit. The mom, who'd been sitting by the window, herded her kids out of the front entrance. Soon, George was the only person left. *Good*.

She focused on Nathan. "What happened? What went wrong?"

He sniffled. Holding the weapon with one hand, he wiped his nose with the other.

George inched to her right. She wanted to clear the counter. Maybe a sane woman would use the espresso machine for cover, but there was something about him. She got the impression that she was seeing the real Nathan Wells for the first time. Maybe she could talk him down and get him to confess. She just needed to play for time. Liam would be here soon. He would call in a tactical team. Knowing Mia, she was probably recording this whole conversation on Liam's phone. All George had to do was keep Nathan talking. "Sometimes it helps to talk about it."

"She was leaving me. She said all the sneaking around was making her feel bad. I agreed to divorce Elizabeth." He swayed forward and then back again, rubbing the hem of his jacket with his free hand.

"Elizabeth said the money was hers and you wouldn't get any." George cleared the counter and took a step closer.

"That's not true. The property she had when we first married was hers, but everything she made after would be divided between us."

His statement was more detailed than she'd expected. "How do you know that?"

"My lawyer told me." He made eye contact with her, and for the first time since he'd entered the café, his mind seemed clear.

"Had you started divorce proceedings?"

"Yes." There was no hesitation in his answer.

That could be easily checked, but George believed him. "How did Elizabeth feel about that?"

"She didn't care. She's a cold bitch." Tears dribbled down his cheeks. "Carly was different. She wanted to be a teacher. She loved kids. She was all heart."

George took another step closer. "Yes, she was. When did you last see Carly alive?"

"We spent Sunday night at the golf course."

"Was that usual?" Another step.

"No, she normally drove back to the city on Sunday afternoon, but she decided to take Monday off to celebrate."

"Celebrate what?"

"My divorce." He had been waving his arms as he talked but then pointed the gun at her again, making her stop.

"Did you lose your temper with her? Did your wife show up?"

"No, nothing like that. You have to believe me. I didn't kill her." His voice held a whiny, desperate tone.

"What happened?" George was about three steps from him, but there was still a small table between them.

"I went to get breakfast." He pointed his weapon at the glass case. "Some muffins and coffee. When I got back, she was dead. It was horrible." He stifled a sob.

"What did you do then?"

"I called Stilton."

"Why not the police?

"I don't know. I wasn't thinking." He blinked rapidly. "Stilton said we had to get rid of her body because people would think I did it. And he was right, wasn't he? You think I killed her."

George heard the electronic buzzer, telling her someone had entered the coffee shop. She ignored it, focusing on Nathan.

He was their prime suspect because he'd lied to them from the beginning, even going so far as to buy a phone. "You sent the text from an imaginary new boyfriend. Did you clear out her dorm room, too?

"Yes," he wailed, his pain coming to the surface.

"What did you do with her stuff? Did you throw it away?"

"No, it's in storage. I would never throw it out." He wept and pressed his hands to his face, the weapon butting against his runny nose.

"You need to put down the gun. What would Carly want you to do?"

"She would want me to join her." Nathan turned the handgun toward his chest.

"No, don't." George scrambled around a table and managed to kick his arm.

A loud boom ricocheted through the coffee shop as the gun discharged. Bits of plaster rained down on her head. Nathan jerked, his body twitching as he fell to the floor, spasming.

Liam stood behind him, a discharged taser in his hand. He stared at George in disbelief. "Why would you run toward a man with a gun?"

CHAPTER THIRTY-ONE

George nursed a mug of stale coffee. Liam had driven her to the Magpie Police Station and had accompanied her to his office. There, he'd wrapped a blanket around her shoulders and then left to deal with the crime scene at the Jumping Bean.

Jake appeared in the door with a plate piled with sandwiches. "A kind member of the public delivered these."

"Let me guess, Randy Woychuk." George slipped the blanket off her shoulders, stood, and took the dish from Jake. She wasn't hungry, but it would've been rude to leave Jake standing there.

"How did you know?" Jake gave her a quizzical look.

"That man seems to think food cures all." She remembered last Wednesday, nearly a week ago, when Randy had persuaded her to pay a visit to Susan Hale. "Have you heard from Liam?"

"He called to see how you were doing, but that's all." Jake shrugged.

"Are Anna Wiebe and Bruce Koval in custody here?"

"Yes, why?" Jake's eyes narrowed, seemingly suspicious of her.

She didn't answer his question but instead asked another one. "And Elizabeth Wells?"

"They're questioning her now."

"I don't think she'll be any help. They need to talk to the other two."

Jake's eyes widened. "Is this the kind of information I should pass on to the boss?"

"Oh, yes. You need to call Liam and tell him. I don't think Nathan or Elizabeth killed Carly.

****

Liam marched into his office with Mia by his side. Georgina sat in a chair with a blanket around her shoulders and her eyes closed, napping.

125

They were holding Elizabeth Wells for questioning, but she wasn't very forthcoming. And he had to admit there was no evidence to suggest she had anything to do with Carly's death, just a pair of earrings she claimed to have found in her husband's truck.

"Mia, have your people found any cameras or listening devices in the golf course apartment?" Georgina asked without opening her eyes.

"Hold on, I'll ask." Mia stepped out of the office to make a call. If she was surprised that Georgina was awake, she didn't show it.

"What's this about?" Liam paced to the window to stare out at the darkness. He was too tense to sit. The vision of Nathan Wells with his weapon aimed at Georgina had chilled him to his core.

Georgina opened her eyes, stood, and stretched. "Olivia told me that no matter what the town council is voting on, Anna Wiebe always comes out on top. It always works in her favor."

Mia walked into the office without knocking. "The techs found two. Both were small with no Wi-Fi capability."

Georgina nodded as she stared blankly into the distance. "Mia, I suggest you ask the mayor if your people can sweep the town hall, Anna Wiebe's place of work, and anywhere she frequents for cameras and listening devices."

"You think she was bugging people?" Liam failed to see what this had to do with Carly's death.

Georgina ran her hands through her long, dark hair, her frustration with them evident. "Yes, remember Stilton said she always visited the apartment at the golf course on Monday mornings."

Liam slapped his forehead. God, he was slow. "She had to download the cameras so she could blackmail people."

Georgina rubbed her temples, her sadness and fatigue evident. "Nathan told me that he left Carly there on Monday morning to go and get breakfast. By the time he returned, she was dead. I believe him."

126

"Carly caught Anna Wiebe retrieving her hidden cameras," Mia hissed, suppressing her burst of excitement. She finally understood how the pieces fit together.

Georgina nodded, her eyes dull. "The Carly I knew wouldn't have kept quiet about blackmail. She would've called me."

"Anna Wiebe killed Carly so she could keep blackmailing people." Liam could see the hurt and despair in Georgina's eyes, but also the relief in knowing why Carly had died. She was dealing with a lot.

Mia pulled out her phone again. "Okay, I'll get the appropriate warrants. Although, I'm pretty sure your mayor will give us permission for the searches." She nodded at Georgina. "Good work." She left the room again to make her calls.

Liam tugged Georgina into his embrace. He wanted her to know she could lean on him. "You're the smartest person I've ever met."

Georgina buried her face in his chest for a moment before she looked up at him. "Not really. I knew Carly. Everyone kept saying she was after the money, but the woman I knew was not like that. To be honest, I should have seen it sooner. When Nathan was in the Jumping Bean with his gun, he confirmed what I knew to be true."

"That Carly was a good person."

"Yes, and she wasn't after the money. In fact, she was the only person in this whole thing who was honest." Her voice trembled.

"Even Nathan was cheating on his wife," Liam said, confirming her assessment.

"And so was Koval, which was why Anna Wiebe was able to manipulate him into coming here and telling you to back off."

He rubbed his hands along her spine, wishing he could do something to make her pain go away. "I'm going to be here into the wee hours. I'll ask Greg to give you a ride home."

She gave him a peck on the lips. "I'll keep the bed warm for you."

CHAPTER THIRTY-TWO

Anna Wiebe had the audacity to smile and wave at Liam as he entered the interrogation room with Mia by his side.

"Bruce Koval will testify that you were blackmailing him. That's one charge of extortion under the criminal code," Mia stated. She hadn't introduced herself.

Anna Wiebe wore the same expensive bright red coat she had the day they'd met at the Wells' house. She put a hand to her chest and blinked her long, mascaraed lashes, faking her shock.

Liam continued, laying out what they could prove, "James Stilton will testify you were there at the time of Carly's death and that he left his hammer in the kitchen area of the apartment."

Anna Wiebe gasped, but it struck Liam as show and not real emotion.

Mia glanced down at her notebook and said, "We have searched your house and seized all your electronic devices. We are also calling in a forensic accountant to go over your finances. They will work in tandem with the Alberta Ombudsman to see how many projects you benefited from as a member of the council. The investigation will be a long one. The Crown Prosecutor has requested seizure of all your assets."

She thumped the table. "You can't do that."

Mia smiled. It was the grin of a predator who knew their prey was trapped. If Anna Wiebe had any sense, she would be scared. "We also have the cameras from the attic apartment. I especially like the wall mount clock. It looks so plain and ordinary. No one would ever guess that there's a lens in the number six on the dial. It only has one drawback, doesn't it?" Mia took a pause and then said. "The wall clock doesn't have WI-FI capability. You can't see the video unless you go there in person and retrieve the SD card.

"Here's what I think. You went to check your cameras in the golf club apartment like you did every Monday, but you weren't expecting Carly to be there. I'm thinking she probably surprised you as you were taking the SD card out of the clock. I've got to hand it to you. That's a cool piece of equipment. It's so inconspicuous." She turned to Liam. "Even we overlooked it the first time we were in the apartment, didn't we?"

Liam nodded.

Anna Wiebe stared at them, her face pale. Her arms were clasped tight across her chest. Perhaps the reality of her situation had finally sunk in.

"We know from blood splatter evidence that Carly was killed in the bedroom," Mia continued. "Which means you bumped into her in the bedroom, then left the room and walked to the kitchen where you grabbed the hammer out of Stilton's toolbox. You then returned and hit her three times. Do you have anything to add?"

"I'm innocent. I didn't do it."

"The Crown Prosecutor will be laying charges." Mia pushed her chair away from the table and stood.

Liam followed. The satisfaction in apprehending Carly's killer was mixed with the depressing knowledge that she had just been in the wrong place at the wrong time, and an evil extortionist decided she had to die.

It was all such a waste.

CHAPTER THIRTY-THREE

Two Weeks Later

George gasped as she walked into the bright yellow kitchen of the Osborne house. "The first thing we'll have to do is paint."

Liam raised an eyebrow. "It's eye-catching, isn't it?"

"That's one way of putting it." George squinted. "It makes me want to wear sunglasses."

Their offer to purchase the place had been accepted, and although they hadn't taken possession yet, the current owners had allowed them access so they could compile a list of improvements they wanted to make.

The home wasn't as big, or as run-down, as she imagined. The front entrance opened into the living room. There were two full bathrooms, which had both been updated. But the color scheme was mind-boggling. It was like a psychedelic trip into the sixties. There were purple, green, bright blue, and brown walls. The whole place needed painting.

Liam stared up at the ceiling. "I know how to change the light fixtures so that will save some money."

"I like the hardwood floors on the main floor, but I want to pull up the shag-pile carpet in the bedrooms, even if we just replace it with a cheap laminate for now." George scribbled her thoughts in her notebook.

Liam frowned. "Don't you want to change the kitchen cabinets first? We don't have the money to do both."

He had a point. The cabinetry was the same bright yellow as the walls.

"That rug is so old. I dread to think of the dirt, stains, and mold that have accumulated over the years." She pulled out a drawer and examined it, checking for any sign that it was made of particle board, a wood product that didn't last as long as solid wood. "It's been a while, but I've refinished tables and such. We could paint the cabinets white and buy new doors. That should save us some cash."

He gave her a thumbs up. "I forgot you used to fix up old furniture. Okay, let's do that."

A knock sounded at the door. "Hello." Mia stepped into the living room. "This place is..." She glanced at the bright green walls of the living room, probably searching for something diplomatic to say. "Nice."

"What are you doing here?" Liam demanded, undoubtedly surprised at her presence.

She rolled her eyes. "For God's sake, I'm not keeping tabs on you. I was in the area and thought I'd give you an update on the Hale case. I saw that piece of junk you call a car parked outside and put two and two together. Georgina isn't the only one who can do deductive reasoning, you know."

"What's the news?" George asked. Both she and Liam had attended Carly's funeral two days ago. Her eyes were still red, swollen and sore from crying.

"Anna Wiebe is pleading guilty to manslaughter."

Liam snorted. "She's getting off easy."

"Agreed, but her case meets the 'suddenness' aspect that has to be present for manslaughter. She didn't go to the golf course with a plan to kill Carly. But she's also been charged with extortion. It's too early to tell, but I suspect more charges will be laid once the Alberta Ombudsman has finished their investigation."

"What about Nathan and Elizabeth Wells?" George asked.

"Nathan Wells and James Stilton have both been charged with illegally disposing of a dead body. That carries a maximum sentence of five years."

"And Elizabeth?" Liam pressed.

"There's no evidence to indicate she was involved with Carly's death." Mia inhaled and then said, "But permission for her condo development in Magpie has been put on hold pending an investigation."

George worked the kinks out of her shoulders to release her tension. "That's good news. I know Olivia will be pleased."

"There is one other thing." Hesitating, Mia pressed her lips into a grim line. Finally, she said, "We got away with Georgina's involvement in the case because she's still, technically, a member of the Magpie Police Service."

"I feel a 'but' coming," Liam muttered.

"This can't happen going forward. Once her sick leave runs out, she can't have any input on cases unless you make her an auxiliary officer."

"There's an idea." Liam gave Mia a slow grin. "I like it."

"A what?" George asked.

Mia grinned like she'd won a pie-eating contest. "It would solve the problem, should it arise again."

"What would solve the problem?" George hated that she didn't understand what they were talking about.

Liam nodded. "And the local school called about her drug presentations. She could still do them."

George thumped the living room wall to get their attention. "What is an auxiliary police officer?"

Liam smiled. "An auxiliary officer has the authority to enforce the criminal code as long as they are working alongside a regular police officer."

"It means Liam can use you, if needed, on investigations. He could justify your presence as his note taker. You would wear your uniform, which should stop any questions about your status."

"Can I still work in the coffee shop?" Olivia had offered George a part-time paid position at the Jumping Bean. She'd accepted the offer.

"Oh, yes, this would be a volunteer position only. You wouldn't be paid."

George nodded. "Okay, I'll do it. But I don't think it's really necessary. I mean, how many more cases are there going to be in a small town like Magpie?"

IF YOU ENJOYED THREE FOR A GIRL

**You can read other books in
The Magpie Romantic Suspense Mysteries
One For Sorrow
&
Two For Joy**

**You might Also enjoy Marlow's
Gathering Storm Series**

SIGN UP FOR MARLOW'S
NEWSLETTER TO HAVE

two Gathering Storm stories delivered to your inbox.
You'll also be notified of sales and new releases.
You can unsubscribe at any time.
https://www.subscribepage.com/marlowkelly

"THE CHEMISTRY BETWEEN THE MAIN CHARACTERS IS OUT OF THIS FREAKING WORLD!"

5 star
Amazon review for
Disturbance